'What do you want with me?'

'I need your presence for a few days. For business purposes.'

'You may need my presence,' Lora said coldly, 'but I would much rather do without yours.'

To her astonishment Luc laughed. 'I admire your spirit and I like the way your eyes sparkle when you get angry, but you have just broken the first rule of kidnapping...'

'What's that?' she asked suspiciously.

'Never insult your kidnapper!'

D1740521

Sally Carr trained as a journalist and has worked on several national newspapers. She was brought up in the West Indies and her travels have taken her nearly all over the world, including Tibet, Russia and North America. She lives with her husband, two dogs, three goldfish and six hens in an old hunting lodge in Northamptonshire, and has become an expert painter and decorator. She enjoys walking, gardening and playing the clarinet.

Recent titles by the same author:

DECEPTIVE DESIRE

A
CAPTIVE HEART

BY
SALLY CARR

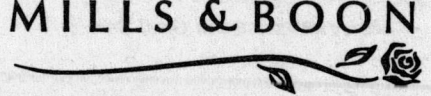

MILLS & BOON

DID YOU PURCHASE THIS BOOK WITHOUT A COVER?

If you did, you should be aware it is **stolen property** as it was reported *unsold and destroyed* by a retailer. Neither the Author nor the publisher has received any payment for this book.

All the characters in this book have no existence outside the imagination of the author, and have no relation whatsoever to anyone bearing the same name or names. They are not even distantly inspired by any individual known or unknown to the author, and all the incidents are pure invention.

All rights reserved. The text of this publication or any part thereof may not be reproduced or transmitted in any form or by any means, electronic or mechanical, including photocopying, recording, storage in an information retrieval system, or otherwise, without the written permission of the publisher.

This book is sold subject to the condition that it shall not, by way of trade or otherwise, be lent, resold, hired out or otherwise circulated without the prior consent of the publisher in any form of binding or cover other than that in which it is published and without a similar condition including this condition being imposed on the subsequent purchaser.

*MILLS & BOON and the Rose Device
are trademarks of the publisher.
Harlequin Mills & Boon Limited,
Eton House, 18-24 Paradise Road, Richmond, Surrey TW9 1SR
This edition published by arrangement with
Harlequin Enterprises B.V.*

© Sally Carr 1995

ISBN 0 263 79056 8

*Set in Times Roman 10 on 12 pt.
01-9507-52120 C1*

Made and printed in Great Britain

CHAPTER ONE

LORA reached her hands up to the ceiling and let the shower play over her body. 'I'm in France,' she told herself. 'Actually here on my first ever business trip.' And then, reaching for the soap, she began to carol loudly and untunefully what she could remember of *'Alouette, gentille alouette'*.

It was not until she regretfully turned off the shower that she heard the hammering at the door. Pulling on a bathrobe and running a hand through her slicked-back blonde hair, she walked through to her bedroom and listened in astonishment to the noise.

'All right, I'm coming, there's no need to break the door down,' she called, reaching for the handle. 'I...' But whatever she had been going to say died on her lips as she gazed at the stranger filling up her doorway.

He was not handsome in any classical sense, but he certainly had presence. And a pair of black eyes that she guessed could be as soft as velvet, but which were now looking her up and down with a mixture of astonishment and calculation.

'Are you Room Service or something?' she asked tentatively. 'Because I haven't ordered anything.'

The black eyes held their first glint of amusement. 'I am not Room Service, *mademoiselle*. Therefore I must, as you say, be ''something''.'

He was certainly that all right, Lora silently agreed as she looked at him again. He watched her as if knowing

5

exactly what she was thinking and then asked with studied politeness, 'May I speak with Lora Seaton, please?'

'You're speaking to her.'

'Really?' he said, raising his eyebrows. 'You are truly Miss Seaton? Of Carrington Enterprises?'

Lora drew herself up to her full height of five feet three inches. Why did people never seem to take her seriously? 'Of course I am, and if it comes to that,' she demanded, 'who are you?'

'I thought you were perhaps Miss Seaton's secretary,' he shrugged, ignoring her question. 'You look so... unsophisticated for a businesswoman.'

Lora's eyes sparked. She might be young but she didn't have to stand for this sort of patronising treatment. Especially not from a complete stranger. She stalked to her dressing-table, glared at herself in the mirror and stalked back.

'Yes, it's definitely me, Lora Seaton,' she said coldly. 'I just checked. And I have no assistant. Now if that's it I'd be grateful if you stated your business and then disappeared as quickly as you came. Whatever you're selling, I don't want it.'

The faintly amused look in his eyes was too much. He looked at her as if she were an ant which had asked him to move to one side. She made to shut the door, but he put his hand out and held it open.

'What the...?' exclaimed Lora. She looked at the stranger's bland expression and assumed a bravery she did not feel. 'If you're not gone in ten seconds I shall call the hotel manager,' she declared, trying to steady the quiver in her voice.

'No need,' replied the man. 'I am the owner.'

Lora looked in bewilderment at him. 'You're not some kind of salesman?' she said faintly, knowing even as she spoke that the answer would be no. Salesmen always seemed to care about other people's opinions, and it was becoming all too obvious to Lora that this man wouldn't give tuppence what anyone thought of him. 'Will you please tell me what is going on?' she added.

'Certainly,' said the stranger. 'It seems that I owe you an apology.'

Lora's hand fell limply from the doorknob as she gazed at him. He stared back impassively. 'Apology?' she echoed uncomprehendingly. This must be some kind of joke. 'What for?' she demanded, determined to get some sort of a reaction out of him. 'You don't look as though you've ever apologised to anyone in your entire life.'

'Well,' he shrugged, 'there is always a first time.' He smiled at her again and she fought down the impulse to smile back. The soft eyes held hers and she suddenly felt as if she was drowning in their depths. 'Miss Seaton,' he said gently, 'don't you want to know what I am going to apologise for?'

'What?' With a start she realised that she had spent the last thirty seconds just staring at this extraordinary man. She gave her head a little shake. 'I'm sorry,' she improvised. 'Jet-lag affects me really badly.'

His lips twitched. 'Yes,' he sympathised. 'One hour spent flying over the English Channel is enough to put anybody out of sorts.

'Now——' he assumed a businesslike tone '—how about letting me in? Or do you want me to make my confession out here in the hall?'

He stood in the middle of the small room, his height making it seem even smaller, his eyes taking in everything—the half-unpacked overnight bag, the clothes she had kicked off in a trail to the bathroom and then Lora herself. She pulled the robe more closely around her body.

'You said you had an apology to make,' she said crossly. 'Not a full-scale inspection.'

He glanced once more round the room. 'You are not a very tidy person, *mademoiselle*.'

'Well, I'm not applying for a job as the hotel chambermaid,' retorted Lora.

His eyes glinted. 'I was merely reflecting that it is a shame you have gone to all this trouble when you will just have to pack everything up again.'

'Pack?' repeated Lora. 'But I'm here for a couple of days.'

'Unfortunately not,' said the stranger smoothly. 'That is what I've come to apologise about. This room has been double-booked.'

'Well, hard luck,' said Lora impatiently. 'I'm here and I'm staying here. Apart from any other considerations, the town seems to be packed out at the moment and I couldn't find a room anywhere else at all.'

The man shrugged. 'We have a very old couple coming to stay. They are always put in these rooms because they are the quietest and the lift is so near. There was a mix-up with your booking, and I admit I am relying on your good nature to give up this room, but I would not dream of putting you out on the street.'

'Very nice of you, I'm sure,' replied Lora drily.

'They really are a very nice old couple,' he said gently. 'I would hate to disappoint them. I'm sure you would too.'

She looked once more into his eyes and felt her resolve weakening. 'Oh, all right,' she sighed. 'But I'm not going to be shoved into some attic room.'

'Certainly not,' he said. 'There is an excellent room free at my other hotel. It is on the other side of town and, if anything, it is slightly better than this one. If you could pack your bags now I will take you there myself.'

'Now?' said Lora, astonished. 'But I've only just got here.'

He shrugged. 'I told you I needed to apologise.'

Those eyes of his were almost irresistible. With a start she realised that he was talking to her again. 'I could send someone to help you pack if you like.'

Lora looked at her underwear strewn all over the floor and felt her face flame. 'No, thanks, I'm perfectly capable,' she snapped, knowing full well that he was quite aware of her confusion. What on earth was getting into her?

'I shall be waiting for you in the lobby,' he said, turning to go.

'All right,' she agreed. 'I'll be there in half an hour.'

His eyes glinted. 'Ten minutes should be ample,' he said. 'After all, it wouldn't do to keep that nice old couple waiting.'

She fought back the impulse to throw her hairbrush at him and with a final smile he turned and left. She sat limply on her bed, her mind in a whirl, gazing numbly at the door closing behind him. What a man. What an extraordinary, arrogant, infuriating man.

He was at the reception desk with the manager when she eventually walked down the stairs to the foyer. 'Ready?' He smiled amiably at her as she handed over the key.

'As I'll ever be,' sighed Lora.

He picked up her case as if it were as heavy as a paper bag and carried it outside to his waiting Mercedes. 'Goodbye,' called the manager behind her. 'And good luck!'

The owner did not turn around but he lifted a hand in acknowledgement and Lora stared, perplexed, at his back. Why should the manager be wishing them good luck?

But before she even had time to frame the question she was sitting in the car's front passenger seat watching him pull out into the town's sleepy traffic.

'Excuse me,' she said after a few minutes, 'Monsieur Whatever-your-name-is, but didn't we just pass the other hotel?'

He shot her a sideways glance. 'We did, yes,' he agreed at last.

'Well, isn't that where we're going?'

'No,' he replied.

Little alarm bells began to ring all through Lora's nervous system.

'You are a hotelier?' she asked nervously.

Again a sideways glance. He shrugged a typically Gallic shrug, his eyes unfathomable pools.

'Aren't you?' Lora insisted, her blood chilling. What was happening to her?

'I have decided to take you to other accommodation,' he said at last.

'Let me out of this car this minute,' insisted Lora. 'I want to go back to town. I have an important property contract to sign tomorrow and——' She broke off, suddenly struck by the full implications of what was happening.

'I hate to disappoint you,' he said, 'but I will not be taking you back to town. You could say that I am a temporary kidnapper. Yours.'

Lora sat back in her seat as though she had had all the breath knocked out of her. To be taken from civilisation, from normality, to the strange and frightening unknown was unthinkable. It happened occasionally to other people that she read about in newspapers. But now it had happened to her. She looked at the stranger and swallowed.

He was wearing a well-cut dark suit, the epitome of civilised man, but it served only to accentuate his lean, well-muscled body. And his face, intent on the road ahead, was obviously that of someone accustomed to getting what he wanted.

'What do you want with me?' she said at last. 'My family couldn't afford to pay a ransom. And they'll be so worried. I——' She bit back the sob in her voice. She had to act calmly.

The car slowed as the stranger grasped one of her hands. Lora almost cried out at the unexpected contact, but his grip was oddly comforting. 'There will be no ransom demand,' he said softly. 'Your family will not be worried in any way. It is simply that I need your presence for a few days. For business purposes.'

Lora withdrew her hand from his grasp and sat up as tall as she could. 'You need my presence,' she said coldly, 'but I would much rather do without yours.'

To her astonishment he laughed. 'You have just broken the first rule of kidnapping,' he said.

'What's that?' she asked suspiciously.

'Never insult your kidnapper!' he answered. 'But I admire your spirit. Insult me some more—I like the way your eyes sparkle when you get angry.'

Lora pursed her lips and stared at him. How arrogant could a man get? She suddenly remembered an article she had read about kidnapping. Hadn't some expert said it was vital for the victim to try to keep up a rapport with the captor? 'Build some sort of relationship and he might think twice about killing you.' The words came flooding back all too vividly and Lora swallowed. 'I don't even know your name,' she said stiffly.

'No,' he replied. 'A terrible social disadvantage for you, I agree, but perfectly acceptable to me, in the circumstances.'

This was no good at all. 'I must call you something,' she said desperately.

He shrugged again. 'I would have thought you would have called me plenty of names by now.'

'Why should I stoop to your level?' retorted Lora.

He glanced at her briefly and smiled. '*Touché*,' he said, and then, concentrating once more on the road, he added, 'My name is Luc.'

Lora looked around at the countryside they were passing. Vineyard after neat vineyard stretched away in all directions. The heart of the Gironde. They could only be ten kilometres at the most from St Emilion, which would be full of tourists buying the area's world-famous claret, full of people leading normal lives, completely oblivious to her plight as she was driven past the hill-top town.

It was late evening now, and darkness was beginning to shade the sky. The beginnings of a plan of escape began filtering through her brain. It was madness, but she had to try it.

Her chance came as a tractor pulled out of one of the fields directly in front of the car. Luc muttered something short and sharp in French and practically stood on the brakes. In that moment, as all his attention was on the road ahead, Lora pulled open her door and threw herself out of the car.

The grassy verge was much harder than it looked and Lora felt as though all the breath had been knocked out of her. She wanted to lie still and let the waves of blackness seeping into her brain take over.

But she had to get up. Had to get up and had to get away. She staggered dizzily to her feet and began making for the town as fast as she could. The trouble was it didn't seem so very fast. And her legs were turning to jelly.

She heard shouts but she kept on going. A hand grasped her arm and she tried to shake it off. 'Go away,' she gasped, but he was in front of her, blocking her way, gripping her elbows and pulling her to him.

'If I went away, you would fall down,' said the husky voice she was beginning to know so well.

She stared wildly at him. 'I don't care,' she yelled. 'I'd rather collapse in a heap than be some kidnap victim. Especially yours.'

He gazed at her, a muscle pulsing in his cheek. 'Mark Todd has a lot to answer for. I would never have thought even he would stoop so low as to send a complete innocent to do his dirty work.'

Lora's jaw dropped. 'You know my boss's name,' she said slowly.

'I know a great many more murky things about Mr Todd than just his name,' Luc replied.

Lora brushed her hair back from her face with an unsteady hand. 'That's rich, coming from you,' she retorted. 'At least he doesn't go around kidnapping complete strangers.'

'That may be true,' conceded Luc. 'I wouldn't like to imagine what he does as light relief from his normal activities.'

Lora opened her mouth to reply but her voice was drowned out by the arrival of the tractor driver. He had jumped down from his machine when she'd made her bid for freedom and now he was stumbling over the verge towards them, waving his arms to heaven and shouting furiously at both her and Luc.

But to her astonishment, as Luc began replying, his expression turned from fury to confusion to, at last, a smiling understanding. He patted them both on the shoulder and as he stood back Luc pulled Lora more closely into his arms. 'What are you doing?' she whispered furiously.

'I'm going to kiss you,' he said. And before she could protest his lips were claiming hers, his hand in her hair, her blood thrilling to the touch of this irresistible, unpredictable stranger.

As he drew away he was smiling at her, and a sudden anger at his arrogance flooded through her. Without even thinking she slapped his face, and was amazed at the burst of laughter behind her. Turning, she could see the tractor driver watching them closely, obviously amused by the pantomime they were providing.

'What is the matter with that man?' Lora demanded.

'I told him we were lovers,' said Luc, thoughtfully rubbing his cheek. 'Of course, when you hit me, that just confirmed it as far as he was concerned.'

Lora's eyes sparked. 'If this is how all Frenchmen behave, I'm not surprised they think it's normal to get their faces slapped. Just who the hell do you think you are?'

In answer he brushed the tips of his fingers down her cheek and smiled slightly at her. 'It is not important, for the time being, who I am,' he said. 'This is neither the time nor the place for frank discussions. How are you feeling?'

'I'm all right,' she replied stiffly.

'You don't look it.'

'Thanks very much,' said Lora. 'Nice of you to say so, I'm sure.'

'You are trembling,' he said softly. 'You have dirt on your face and if you were a child I would have said you were about to burst into tears.'

'Well, I'm not,' retorted Lora, rubbing her hand across her eyes and swallowing fast.

He smiled gently at her. 'Jumping out of the car like that was a very foolish thing to do, but brave. I know it was going slowly but I could have speeded up at any time.' For some reason his sudden softness made her feel closer to tears than ever. He tipped her chin up and stared into her eyes. 'You have my admiration.' And, bending down, he picked her up and carried her back to the car.

She did not even try to protest as he laid her gently on the back seat. 'I don't think you've broken anything,' he said. 'Although I'm no doctor.'

'No,' she replied muzzily. 'You can say that again.'

The rest of the journey was one of dark haziness to Lora. Was she dreaming, or had the car really stopped?

'Wake up, Lora. We have arrived.' She focused slowly on the evening light flooding into the car, to find Luc's eyes six inches from her own. He had opened the back door of the Mercedes and was squatting down by the seat. 'How do you feel?' he asked.

'Terrible,' she said glumly. 'But I expect I'll live.'

He repressed a smile. 'I expect you shall. Can you walk to the house?'

Lora's eyes opened properly. This man must be truly mad. 'We're going for a walk?'

He nodded. 'I'm afraid so. It will be a trek of about five metres. Do you think you can manage such a distance?'

Lora lifted her head and saw that they were parked on a gravel drive outside a grey stone farmhouse. 'You must be the laziest kidnapper ever,' she said slowly. 'What do you really expect me to do? Walk to the house, find the cellar and chain myself up in it?'

He shrugged. 'You can stay in the car, if you like. There is a bedroom all ready for you in the house. It is plain but comfortable. However, if you prefer the idea of sitting in the cellar I won't object.'

Lora blinked. His words were light but it was still obvious that she was his prisoner. The reality of the situation hit her again with full force. 'Are you going to lock me up?' she quavered.

He looked at her speculatively. 'No.'

She swung her legs off the seat and sat up, clutching her head as a momentary wave of dizziness overtook her. 'What happens if I try to run away?'

'Right at this moment you could not even run a bath,' replied Luc flatly. 'And besides, out here there is nowhere for you to run to.'

It had not been so very difficult for Luc to persuade her to get out of the car, she reflected soon after. The soft night air had soothed her throbbing head and the idea of going to bed had proved irresistible. Her room, in the yellow light of a completely inadequate bedside lamp, was, as Luc had said, plain. But it was not without charm. It had a low beamed ceiling and the walls were of a mellow stone. The windows were firmly shuttered. There was a big, high bed in the centre and the rough linen sheets smelled of lavender. 'I'm going to need stepladders to get into that bed,' she breathed.

'It is not that high,' replied Luc. 'It appears so because the mattress is of feathers and has been...' he paused and wrinkled his forehead '...fattened up,' he said at last.

Lora smiled. 'I think you mean plumped,' she corrected him.

He lifted an eyebrow. 'Plumped, then. Never will I get the complete hang of English.'

Lora twisted her lips. It would be so easy to like this man, if it were not for what he had done. But what he had done was too great to forgive.

'Maybe you should kidnap more English people,' she said tartly. 'Concentrate your scale of operations. And then when you get arrested by English police and put in an English gaol I'm sure your vocabulary will improve enormously.'

He reached out and pulled her towards him. 'I would much rather have you than a policeman for a teacher, Lora Seaton,' he said softly.

His fingers stroked through her hair, lifting her face to his. His head dropped and he kissed her throat, tracing a burning path to her lips before pulling back and staring intently at her flushed face. Her heart was beating twice as fast as normal and her breath was coming short and fast. He had absolutely no right to make her feel this way.

She breathed deeply and gazed at him as steadily as she could. 'I'd like to teach you a lesson,' she said, refusing to acknowledge the age-old signs that were pounding through her blood. 'But it wouldn't be in English grammar.'

'Really?' he mused. 'In that case, I am not convinced that you could teach me anything I do not already know.'

Their eyes locked and Lora was the first to look away. Why did he have this effect on her? It was so irritating. So... shaming. She wanted to kick herself for her lack of control.

'Lora, look at me.'

Unwillingly she dragged her eyes to meet his. 'Why should I look at you?' she said defiantly. 'You have taken away my freedom and I hate you.'

'Do you really hate me as much as you say?' His voice was soft, irresistible. She swallowed.

'I think you're despicable,' she muttered. She held herself rigid, not knowing what he was going to do next, and was utterly surprised when he dropped a kiss on the tip of her nose.

'Sweet dreams, Lora.'

It was shocking to feel the sudden sense of disappointment flood over her as he stood back and reached for the door-handle.

Angered by her emotions, she glared at him. 'I must say I can't wish you the same. I hope you have the worst nightmares of your life.'

He gazed at her steadily. 'It is lucky for me I have found you such soothing company. If I have nightmares I shall come to you for comfort.'

Lora bent down and wrenched off one of her stilettos. If she was lucky the heel would skewer him right where it hurt. But when she straightened up to take aim, the door had closed with a soft click.

She stilled for a second as she remembered exactly what had happened to her, before kicking off her other shoe and running to the door. The tattoo she beat out on the rough old wood would have been enough to waken the dead. 'Let me out!' she yelled. 'Let me out!' But there was no reply and, sobbing wretchedly, she turned and threw herself full-length on the bed.

Later, much later, so that it was almost as if she were dreaming, the door opened again and soft footsteps came near. A cool hand brushed her forehead. Why did she feel so feverish? Restlessly she moved on the bed. It wasn't fair for a dream to be so uncomfortable. Murmuring, she lifted her arms out in mute appeal and again those cool hands were sliding over her skin, magically removing her rucked-up dress.

She sighed and smiled as the cool sheets were pulled over her. She reached out and clasped a hand, but it gently withdrew. 'Don't go away,' she muttered indistinctly. 'Nice dream.'

'Sleep well,' came a familiar husky voice. And then all was silence again as Lora fell into a completely deep sleep.

*　　*　　*

She woke in darkness but she had the distinct feeling that it was late in the day. For a moment she thought she was in the hotel bedroom and then the events of the previous evening came flooding back. Easing herself from the bed, she made her way to the window and pulled open the shutters.

The sunshine was shocking and she blinked her eyes several times. The light wasn't like this in London. It flooded over her and into the room in one glorious wave and she found herself stretching into the light like a cat in front of a gas fire.

She closed her eyes in pleasure and then snapped them open at the realisation that she was not alone. There outside, sitting by a swimming-pool, was her kidnapper, Luc. He was staring at her with a half-smile on his face and, when she gazed back, lifted his hand in mock-salute.

'Good morning,' he called. 'Are you going to join me for breakfast?'

She looked at him narrowly. 'Do I have any choice?'

He shrugged. 'No. Not really. Although you could always go without if you felt you had to make some sort of statement. You know—never eat with your kidnapper; it saps your moral fibre—that sort of thing.'

'What happens if I go without?' she snapped.

He spread his hands. 'You will go hungry.'

She leant over the windowsill. 'Has anyone ever told you exactly what you are?'

He grinned. 'But of course. I would be glad to hear your version, though. I'm sure it would be most educational.

'Shall I order croissants for you, or do you prefer toast? I have marmalade, hot coffee, and even, if you wish, cornflakes. What more could a girl want in the morning?'

His voice was light, teasing, and loaded with double meaning. For one wild instant Lora wanted to smile back at him and then she stilled, realising she was wearing only her underwear, slammed the shutters and scrambled back to bed.

She could feel her cheeks flaming in the darkness as she remembered the 'dream' she had had. If only she could remember it more clearly. But try as she might she could think of nothing more than the touch of his cool hands on her hot skin. Why hadn't she woken up properly and told him exactly where to get off?

Swearing softly, she blasted herself for her weakness. How could you find a kidnapper charming? He was nothing more than a criminal, and one who pursued a truly heartless business.

Lora huddled under the thin sheet. What did he want with her? And who was he? As the minutes ticked by it became increasingly obvious that there was only one way she was going to find out. She was going to have to accept his invitation to breakfast.

She had expected to be in France for two days and her assignment had been a simple one—to visit a lawyer—the *notaire*—and to sign various papers. She had chosen her smartest suit for the job, and it was only now obvious that it was going to be far too hot for this part of France in July. But by wearing it, Lora reasoned, she would not be making any concessions to a man who, however charming, was still her captor. Besides, she'd ruined her only other outfit leaping out of his car.

The thought of her appointment with the *notaire* made her look at her watch in horror. Mark had been most insistent that she be at the man's office at eleven a.m. on the dot. And it was now two p.m. Two o'clock! What was she going to do?

Luc gazed at her over the top of his newspaper as she walked out of the house in her navy blue wool suit with her hair swept back severely.

'Are you coming to breakfast?' he enquired gently. 'Or are you slapping me with a take-over bid?'

Lora pursed her lips. It was impossible to wrong-foot this man. He was too self-assured. Too bloody arrogant. And, a secret voice added, too charming.

She glared at him. 'Don't make any funny remarks,' she snapped. 'I'm here against my will, as you well know.'

He put down his paper and handed her a plate of croissants. 'Bread?' he asked politely.

She took one of the warm brown crescents and ripped it crossly. 'I want to know what I'm doing here,' she demanded.

'Butter?' he added gently, putting a pat on her plate.

She took her knife and dug savagely into the soft yellow gold. 'Don't think you can butter me up with all this display of good manners, Luc. You're a criminal and you're keeping me from my business.'

'Butter you up?' he repeated softly. 'That is a new phrase on me. Is it some sort of exciting invitation?'

She put down her knife with a clatter. 'Don't give me that ignorant Frenchman act,' she said, feeling herself starting to blush. 'You speak with hardly a trace of accent and even that sounds a bit American. I expect you think it's smart to sound like some gangster in a silly film——'

Lora stopped suddenly, appalled at her own bravado. This man could be a killer, anything. She should be trying to be conciliatory, not losing her temper.

His eyes glinted. 'I applaud you for your perception, Lora. I lived for some time in America, but I rarely visited a cinema.'

'I expect you were in gaol,' she retorted, immediately wanting to bite her tongue again. What was the matter with her?

He picked up a croissant with his long brown fingers and looked at her thoughtfully. 'I suppose you could say I was in a prison of a sort. Except all the bars were gold.'

CHAPTER TWO

LUC poured coffee into a ridiculously large cup and added warm milk. 'Here,' he said. 'Drink this.'

She looked at it suspiciously. 'Nobody could possibly drink that much coffee.'

'In France we do,' he said. 'It is good for you. Drink.'

Lora had to admit that the smell was delicious. 'It could be poisoned,' she said doubtfully.

He sat back in his chair and shrugged. 'As you like. But I did not go to all the trouble of kidnapping you just so I could kill you with some spiked coffee.'

Lora lifted the cup with both hands and drank. Her senses had not been wrong. It was delicious. She stared at her captor over the rim and realised that he was wearing nothing but a pair of brief swimming-trunks. Black against the deep tan of his body.

She had been so focused on his personality that she had not, until this moment, even noticed what he was wearing. Now she could not seem to stop herself staring at his flat chest and long, sprawling legs.

He was smiling at her, damn him, and she dropped her eyes hurriedly. By rights she should feel superior, she thought crossly, because she was fully dressed. But he looked so arrogant and self-assured lounging there in his chair. All she could feel was the sweat trickling down her spine and the sun blazing on her head.

'How old are you, Lora?' he asked.

'Twenty-two,' she replied automatically.

'Can you speak French?'

She shook her head wordlessly.

'Has it occurred to you at all why a girl of twenty-two who can't speak French has been sent here to France on a so-called business trip?'

'Mark was short-staffed,' Lora said.

'Knowing him, that does not surprise me at all,' replied Luc.

'What gives you the right to say such rotten things about my boss?' Lora demanded.

Luc shrugged. 'Because they are true,' he said simply. 'Mark Todd is not the sort of man I would trust with a used Metro ticket. And I am amazed he sent someone like you to do his business. Does he have some sort of a hold on you?'

'He hasn't got any sort of hold,' said Lora hotly, all too aware suddenly of the possibilities which Luc's razor-sharp mind was considering. There was a cold feeling in the pit of her stomach as she thought of the last time she had seen Mark Todd. If her present situation weren't so serious Luc's question would be almost laughable.

'Even if he did have some sort of hold, as you so delicately put it,' Lora added, 'it wouldn't be any of your damn business.'

She saw the smile start to form on his lips at her vehemence and had the sudden urge to wipe it off. 'And——' she glared at him '—he doesn't know I can't speak French.'

Luc sat forward suddenly. 'You are kidding,' he breathed. 'How come he doesn't know, Miss Full-of-Surprises Seaton?'

'Because I lied,' said Lora primly, trying desperately to stay cool in the full power of those soft, dark eyes.

Luc raised an eyebrow. 'And so now who is the criminal?' he said lightly.

Lora stared at him, remembering with a rush exactly how she came to be with this man. 'I may be a liar but I haven't kidnapped anyone,' she snapped.

He shrugged. 'It is probably only a matter of time before you slide all the way down the slippery slope. After all, I no sooner usher you into my car than you try to cause a major traffic accident.'

Lora's jaw dropped. 'Usher me?' she spluttered. 'Major traffic accident? Why, of all the nerve...'

He smiled challengingly at her. 'I think it was very public-spirited of me to scoop you off the road and put you back in the car after you had given that perfectly innocent tractor driver the shock of his life. Don't you?'

'If you were that public-spirited,' retorted Lora, 'you would have run yourself over.'

He lifted his hands in mock-horror. 'Such violence! Although I confess your ideas would be slightly difficult to carry out, even for me. And I thought you were such a calm, sweet-faced young woman.'

'Calm!' yelled Lora. 'I'd like to give you calm. Permanently!'

Luc leant forward. 'Believe me, Lora, kidnapping you was distasteful to me, but it had to be done. I am just sorry it had to be you.

'But I am intrigued to hear you managed to fool Mark Todd. How did you do it? He may be many things, but he is not stupid.'

Lora looked at him warily. 'I don't see why I should tell you anything,' she said.

He shrugged. 'As you please. It is of no interest to me either way.'

'Everything about Mark Todd seems to interest you,' said Lora. 'Although I can't see why. I bet you'd even like to know what brand of toothpaste he uses.'

Luc gazed at her speculatively, a small smile tugging at the corners of his mouth. 'It is always useful to know things about...people you may meet,' he said carefully. 'But I'm not interested in toothpaste. Personally I'd be very happy if all his teeth fell out.'

'My, my,' said Lora. 'Would I be right in thinking you two aren't exactly the best of friends?'

'Unlike you and he, it would seem,' parried Luc.

Lora's eyes narrowed. 'Mark hired me merely as a general office assistant, to file things and type letters,' she snapped.

'And now you're soaking up the sun on a big business assignment for him,' said Luc. 'That certainly adds up.'

'It's not so silly as all that,' retorted Lora. 'Mark doesn't have a very big office. It's very smart and it's in the City but there's only him and his personal secretary Carole. During my job interview Mark said there were good opportunities for advancement and travel, if I spoke French. So of course I said, *Mais oui, bien sûr.*'

Luc smiled at her. 'But of course you did,' he agreed. 'I must say you have a very good accent.'

Lora bit her lip. Just how had he managed to get her to tell this story? He was too damn persuasive by half.

'Tell me more,' Luc prompted gently. 'I'm beginning to admire your spirit very much.'

She sighed, but he knew most of her story now; he might as well hear the rest. Besides, what harm could it do? 'I needed that job really badly,' she resumed. 'I think I went to about thirty interviews before that and they were all for completely boring dead-end jobs. So when

Mark asked me if I spoke French I just lied. Didn't even think about it. If he'd asked me if I spoke Swahili I would have said yes and hoped for the best. Those four words make up about the only French conversation I'm capable of. Some character said them on a TV show once and they just stuck in my brain.'

'Did you not study French at school?'

'Yes,' said Lora slowly. 'But my teacher told me I was hopeless. He said teaching me French ought to be viewed as an exercise in damage limitation.'

Luc raised an eyebrow. 'He does not sound particularly patient. Were you really that appalling?'

'Yes,' shrugged Lora. 'I was. I found the words far too confusing.

'Anyway,' she went on, 'that was that, really. Mark took me on and I found knowing French wasn't really that vital. He or Carole always took the overseas calls. They insisted on it. They're really both quite secretive.'

'I'll bet,' said Luc grimly.

Lora glanced at him but his face was quite unreadable. 'Well, so,' she continued, 'everything worked out quite all right, really, until Carole got flu. Mark was practically beside himself. It was obvious the deal here was really important, but he got a letter from his bank insisting he see them today. In the end he said I would have to come here in Carole's place. It was just a property contract, he said, but very important. All I was required to do was sign it on his behalf, and did I think I could manage?'

'And of course you replied, "*Mais oui, bien sûr*",' said Luc.

'Yes,' said Lora glumly. 'A business trip, on my own, to France. Most French people seem to speak English and I was determined to get through somehow. I thought it would be such an experience.'

'Well, you were certainly right there,' mused Luc. 'And your appearance has certainly made things easier for me than I expected. But, in truth, I wish he had sent someone else. Like this Carole, perhaps.'

'What's it got to do with you?' demanded Lora. 'What's your part in all this?'

'My part in this is my own business,' said Luc. 'But you, Lora, are too young to be mixed up in it. I would be sorry to see you get hurt.'

She stood up suddenly, angered at the easy way he had got her to tell him her story. And rattled at the implied danger. 'Well, I'm glad to see you're in some sort of moral dilemma,' she spat. 'But if you were really honest about what you feel you would let me go.'

He stared at her. 'I cannot do that, Lora. Not until tomorrow. By then I should be able to take you to the airport to catch your plane.'

'How do you know I'm leaving tomorrow?' breathed Lora. 'Are you psychic, or what?'

Luc shrugged. 'I went through the contents of your handbag while you were asleep.'

'You did what?' she said furiously.

He stood up and Lora stepped back involuntarily.

'What did you expect?' he asked. 'Of course I searched your things. I am not in a position to take any chances, especially not with an employee of Mark Todd. Going through your handbag seemed like a most sensible thing to do.'

He gazed at her blandly. 'After all, I do not know you that well. You could have been carrying a gun and I do not want to be shot full of holes for my pains.'

'Carry a gun?' said Lora, astonished. 'This isn't America, you know. What on earth would I be doing with one of those?'

Luc smiled at her sardonically. 'Warding off kidnappers?'

'A Sherman tank wouldn't have warded you off,' retorted Lora. 'Although it would have been my wish come true to aim one at you.'

'Then let us hope you do not get your wish granted before tomorrow,' replied Luc smoothly. 'Because I will not let you go until then at least.

'The fact that I have your money, ticket and passport is going to make it doubly difficult for you to try anything silly.'

'I will get away from you,' breathed Lora, taking another step back.

'I wouldn't——' But Luc's words came too late. With a scream and a splash Lora had lost her footing and fallen into the swimming-pool.

Water bellied up under her skirt and dragged at the thick wool. It poured into her mouth and down her nose and she felt as though her lungs would burst. Dimly she heard another splash and then strong hands were around her waist, pulling her along. Panic-stricken, she hit out. What was this infuriating man trying to do now—drown her?

She felt his hands disappear and all rational thought left her completely as she sank again. Then she could feel him behind her, his hand cupping her chin, his other arm around her body, pulling her through the water. She kicked and struggled but it made no difference. She was completely in his power.

It seemed an age but was, in reality, only a few moments before Luc got her to the side of the pool. Nimble as a cat, he hauled himself on to the side and then pulled her out.

'My God!' he exclaimed as she bent double and coughed wretchedly. 'Did you want to drown?'

She glared at him. 'I was perfectly all right till you came along and started grabbing me.' It was a black lie, but at that precise moment she didn't give a damn what she told him.

He stared back, his black eyes snapping. 'You were not perfectly all right. You were drowning.'

'It was all your fault,' she retorted. 'You made me fall in, and the way you messed about in the water unnerved me.'

'Unnerved you!' he said exasperatedly. 'Do you know how you have unnerved me, you infuriating woman? I lived in New York for ten years, and never, ever did my heart stop then like it has stopped in the last twenty-four hours. First you throw yourself out of my car and then you try to do away with yourself in my pool. What did you think? That there was a secret escape route in the deep end?'

'It's not funny,' said Lora, squelching back to the breakfast-table. 'My shoes are down there on the bottom of your precious pool. And they're the only pair I've got. They cost me an arm and a leg.'

'Your dip nearly cost you your life,' said Luc quietly.

Lora peeled off her sodden jacket. Her chiffon blouse was plastered to her body and she realised Luc was looking at her in an entirely new way. A ghost of a smile appeared on his grim features and she caught her breath at the message in his eyes. It told of a sexual power that for one split-second she wanted to consume her utterly.

She pushed her hair back from her face and swallowed.

'You can't swim, can you?' he said softly.

'Anyone can swim, I've been told,' she replied stiffly. 'I've just never tried.'

'Except just now,' he pointed out. 'And if things were different maybe I would teach you.'

'Great,' said Lora bitingly, trying hard to cover her conflicting emotions at Luc's presence. 'Get kidnapped and learn to swim. I think I'll write to a TV holiday programme about it.'

It took two swift steps for him to reach her and grab her arms.

'Let me go!' she cried.

'I would like to shake you until your teeth rattle,' he grated. 'What do you think I am? Some cheap criminal who has preyed on you to line his own pockets?'

Lora clenched her jaw. 'You tell me,' she said coldly.

'I am fighting for my birthright,' replied Luc. 'Your capture was unfortunate, but necessary. Don't think for one moment that I am enjoying this situation any more than you.'

'Then let me go,' said Lora quietly.

Almost in answer his hands gripped her more tightly, and then he sighed. 'That I cannot do.'

Lora lifted her chin. 'Then you are nothing more than——'

But before she could continue his mouth stopped hers with a kiss and Lora felt her whole body tremble as he drew her more closely into his arms, desiring her, claiming her.

'We cannot alter this situation, you and I,' said Luc softly at last. 'We are bound together in this by fate, and if you can accept that it will make it more bearable for you.'

She gazed at him silently, her heart thudding. 'Then let me go,' she repeated.

'No, I cannot,' he replied, releasing his grip on her arms. And, turning on his heel, he left her standing in the searing sunshine.

She felt cold, despite the blistering heat, after he left. The water dripped slowly off her body and she stared at the shimmering pool.

Luc had been so right, damn him.' There was no escape. She was his prisoner, even when he walked away and left her. And there was nothing she could do about it.

She reached mechanically for a towel hanging over the back of a chair and then froze as her gaze focused on something beyond the belt of trees that screened the pool area. Something white and grand and imposing.

Looking around to make sure no one was watching her, Lora walked as nonchalantly as she could to the far end of the pool and stared more carefully at what she had seen.

There, between the trees, nestling in the fields of sunflowers like a diamond on yellow silk, was a château: a long, low fairy-tale house with pillars at the front and two round turrets sparkling in the afternoon sunshine.

If only she could get to it and speak to the people who lived there, even if it was just to beg the use of their telephone, she could escape from this impossible situation. And, more importantly, free herself from the influence of an impossible man.

There was a pair of espadrilles by the side of the pool—
Luc's, obviously. She slipped her feet inside them and
giggled suddenly. They were about twice as big as her
feet and looked totally ridiculous.

Still, they would have to do. A wide bare strip of earth
between the fence and the sunflowers looked hard-baked
and rocky and she would never make it in bare feet.
With one quick glance behind her to check that Luc was
nowhere in sight, she walked through the bushes by the
pool, climbed over the single-strand barbed-wire fence,
scrambled down a small bank and made for the château.

It was much further away than it had appeared from
the pool, and seemed to undulate like a reflection on
water in the shimmering heat.

She could feel the sweat trickle down her neck and
under her arms. There was a sore place on her shoulder-
blades where the damp chiffon was rubbing and the hot
heaviness of her wool skirt was driving her mad. Part
of her longed to unfasten the cruelly tight waistband and
chuck the whole thing in the next ditch. Her feet slid
helplessly about in the espadrilles, too, but she stuck
doggedly to her route. Soon she would be in among the
sunflowers and then, if she just kept going straight on,
she was bound to come out facing the château.

The sunflowers, when she got to them, were much
higher than they had looked from the house and closely
planted. The shaggy yellow heads stared blindly at Lora.

She began to have second thoughts about getting in
among them but there seemed no way round. Somehow
she would have to find a way through those scratchy
green stems.

'I wouldn't, if I were you.'

She whipped round to find Luc leaning against a tree by the fence, his thumbs hooked through the loops of his swimming-trunks.

'How did you get there?' she gasped.

'Same way as you did,' he said. 'I saw you climb over the fence from my window.'

'Well, now you can watch me disappear,' responded Lora tartly.

He smiled at her. 'There are spiders in there, you know.'

Lora swallowed. Trust him to hit on her pet hate. 'I'm not afraid of spiders,' she lied.

He sat down on the bare ochre earth and looked up at the shimmering sky. 'Big black and yellow ones. With enormous furry legs,' he added, almost as if to himself. 'They give quite a nasty bite, I believe.'

Lora stopped dead. She turned to face Luc, almost rigid with frustration and fury.

'So you are afraid of spiders,' he said, smiling.

'I am not afraid of them,' she retorted with as much cold dignity as she could muster. 'I just don't like them very much.' Then, lifting her chin, she added, 'But I'd rather take my chances with them than spend any more time with you.'

'Very brave,' nodded Luc. 'But rather pointless. A bit like the charge of the Light Brigade.'

'What do you mean?' demanded Lora.

Luc shrugged. 'You could spend all morning blundering around in those sunflowers and all I would have to do is watch you from up here and meet you wherever you chanced to stumble out. A complete waste of time for both of us. Not to mention a sad waste of all the sunflowers you would trample.'

Lora glared at him and felt like stamping her foot.

'Why don't you come back with me to the villa?' he said gently. 'I won't be keeping you for much longer.'

That did it. Her temper, so long clamped down, began escaping like steam from a pressure cooker. She bent down, took off one of the espadrilles and heaved it at him. He ducked and it hit the tree with a thwack. 'Keeping me!' she yelled. 'You just think I'm some sort of toy, don't you? Some sort of... inconvenience. Well, I've got news for you, Monsieur Luc Whatever-your-name-is: I am at the end of my tether.'

She shucked off the other espadrille and threw it too. Luc caught it easily and grinned at her. 'So I can see,' he said. 'But you are forgetting that the tether belongs to me.'

'Well, I don't belong to you,' she cried. 'And it's time you realised it. Do you know how you have messed things up for me?' She took one furious look at the sunflowers and stalked back to Luc. The stones in the hard earth stubbed her toes and the heat of it, reflected from the sun, burned the soles of her feet. But she held her head up and kept her pace steady. She was damned if she was going to run back to captivity.

He had been absolutely right, damn him. It had been a desperate doomed act trying to escape that way. But it had been worth it. Anything to show him she was going to be far more trouble than he had bargained for—and damn the article she had read in that newspaper about how to treat kidnappers.

He stood up in one fluid movement, waiting for her to reach him. She couldn't help noticing how the sun shone on the hard muscles of his arms and chest, but she shook her head determinedly. It was time to start making him think for a change. 'Have you really thought about what you have done to me?' she demanded.

He quirked an eyebrow. 'Tell me,' he said quietly.

'You're dead right I'll tell you,' she exploded. 'This was my first decent job. My first job with more prospects than just looking after the office coffee money,' she repeated angrily, 'and it wasn't that easy to come by.' She lifted her right hand and shook it under his face.

'I did a two-year course at college and I hated every moment of it. Have you any idea what it's like to stick at something day after day in a stuffy classroom, gazing at one of those blasted blinking computer screens, when all you really want to do is go out into the sunshine and feel it soak through your body?'

'Yes, I do,' he replied.

Lora gave him one burning glance and swept on, 'Well, I stuck at it and I even managed to pass my exams at the end of the course. And do you know what?'

She glared at him but, before he could even reply this time, she immediately answered, 'When I got my certificates at the end of the course I felt really proud of myself. I was even commended for my cheerfulness and sensitive handling of inter-personnel affairs.'

Luc raised an eyebrow, but said nothing. Lora was suddenly hotly aware that she had not phrased the last statement exactly how she had meant. Her anger and embarrassment redoubling, she pressed on.

'Do you know how long it took me to get this job?' she demanded furiously, adding immediately, 'Ten months. And that only because I lied. My first decent job, my first business trip and what happens? You come along, that's what happens.'

His eyes glinted. 'At least you are out in the sunshine today, *chérie*, instead of staring at a "blasted blinking computer screen". Perhaps you should thank me.'

'Thank you?' gasped Lora. 'Well, of all the...'

He looked at her mockingly. 'I take it then that you don't feel any gratitude at all for your deliverance from a stuffy office?'

'What I feel for you, Luc Whatever-your-name-is, is about as far from gratitude as it is possible to get,' Lora grated. 'My clothes are ruined. My best shoes are at the bottom of your pool and I've almost certainly missed my appointment with Mark's French lawyer. You've kidnapped me, and Mark will probably sack me, and I hate you.'

She lifted a leg over the wire fence and Luc put out his hand to steady her, but she shook it off and scrambled up through the bushes, Luc following her to the pool.

She stood by the edge, breathing deeply, trying to calm down. 'Lora?' He was right behind her. She could almost feel his breath on her neck. What right did he have to sound so calm?

'What?' she said stiffly.

He turned her to face him. 'For what it's worth, I really am sorry you have been mixed up in this. But I could see no other way. I never dreamed Mark would send someone like you.'

Lora bit her lip. 'I'm not entirely sure how to take that,' she muttered.

He brushed back the hair on her forehead. 'You are hot,' he said.

'Thanks to you.'

'Oh, Lora,' he replied softly, the light in his eyes belying the tone of his voice. 'And you were telling me how good you were at the inter-personnel relationships.'

'The course didn't cover kidnappers,' she retorted.

'A pity,' he drawled. 'But for now I think we should both cool down. Don't you?' And before she even realised what was happening he encircled her with his arms and leapt with her into the pool.

The plunge into the cool, clean water was such a delicious change from the hot stickiness of her skin that Lora almost forgot to be terrified. And just at the moment when she started to struggle she found herself being held afloat, staring in frank astonishment at Luc's face.

He smiled at her, easily treading water to support them both. 'Are you not afraid?' he asked gently.

She felt the confident way he held her and then realised with a shock that she was completely out of her depth. Her head was above the surface, thanks to Luc, but what would happen if he were suddenly to let go?

'No,' she lied. 'Why on earth should I be afraid?'

Perhaps he just wouldn't care if he drowned her. Panic began to snowball at the thought of all the water beneath her. 'I want to get out,' she said, trying to steady the tremor in her voice.

'Why don't you just swim away, then?' he said with a challenging glint in his eye. 'I'll just get out of your way, shall I?'

'No, don't,' she said abruptly. 'You were quite right. I can't swim.' She averted her eyes from his gaze and stared at the trees over his shoulder. 'Thank you for keeping me afloat,' she said woodenly.

He laughed suddenly. 'You are such a strange woman at times, Lora. So funny with your wide, clear eyes and stiff formalities.'

His fingers brushed her face, leaving a trail of water droplets across her cheek. 'What goes on behind those eyes of yours, Lora? What are you thinking?'

She looked at him full in the face, and swallowed hard. Why did he have to be so attractive? His arms were encircling her, his body moving against hers in the silky, lapping water. She fought down the urge to reach up and brush away a lock of hair that water had plastered to his eyes.

'What am I thinking?' she repeated uncertainly. He nodded, smiling, and she realised with a sudden rush that he knew exactly what was going through her mind.

'I was just wondering how we were staying afloat,' she managed at last. 'I can't believe it takes so little effort.'

'Believe it or not, you are keeping yourself afloat,' he said. 'Just kick a little more with your feet.'

He loosened his grip and moved further back, now holding on to her hands. 'Not bad,' he said critically. 'But your skirt is pulling you down. Take it off.'

'Certainly not,' she protested.

'Why not?' he asked. 'You've taken practically everything else off. Besides, I do not approve of the colour.'

'I'm not asking you to wear it,' she snapped.

He grinned and bobbed underneath the surface. She opened her mouth to protest but water slapped into her face as his hands travelled down to her waist and tugged away the clinging wool. She kicked out furiously as he stripped away her tights too. And then he was in front of her again, wiping the water from his eyes and grinning wickedly at her. 'All gone,' he announced. 'Come, take

off that silly shirt and I will give you your first swimming
lesson.'

'I don't want to take any more clothes off,' said Lora
stiffly, suddenly feeling as out of her depth mentally as
she did physically. It simply wasn't right that he could
get away with this sort of thing. And the way he smiled
at her... Why did she always find herself wanting to
smile back?

He was smiling at her now, still keeping her afloat in
this azure world of water and sky. 'I'm not asking you
to take all your clothes off,' Luc shrugged. 'And even
with your underwear on you are still more covered up
than most of the girls in Cannes.'

'Well, I am not in the habit of prancing around on
beaches semi-naked,' retorted Lora.

'A pity,' he said lazily.

Lora swallowed hurriedly. 'And in case you hadn't
noticed, we are absolutely nowhere near Cannes.'

CHAPTER THREE

'YOU are quite right,' he said. 'The south of France is a long way from here.' He smiled down into her eyes and she was immediately furious with herself for wanting to smile back. 'You must have got top marks for geography at school,' he added, 'even if your computing skills were not all that could be hoped for.'

'We didn't do geography at college,' said Lora, struggling to stop the breathless feeling in her chest at his closeness.

His hand slid around her neck, lightly resting on her shoulder. 'It is scratchy, this shirt of yours. Why do you insist on wearing something so uncomfortable?'

The tips of his fingers lightly brushed the nape of her neck, and her nerve-endings jolted at the message they sent down her spine. Her lips parted and he drew her once more into his embrace, his fingers travelling up under the despised chiffon, moving with a calm assurance over her satin skin. His mouth was claiming hers with a thrilling insistence she was powerless to deny and time hung suspended as, their bodies stilling in mute intensity, they slid as one down through the water.

Gently as a freed butterfly, Lora's shirt, its inadequate buttons at last giving up the ghost, floated slowly and serenely away. With an upward rush their bodies broke the surface at last, shooting into the air in a fountain of spray and surging water. Lora, her lungs concentrating solely on drawing breath, couldn't speak as she swayed in Luc's arms.

'Are you angry with me?' he asked, staring at her sparking eyes. 'Are you going to slap my face and storm off in clouds of fury and insulted virtue?'

Lora pressed her lips together. Somehow she had to get a grip on her emotions before they went completely haywire. 'I think you are the most impossible man I have ever met,' she said at last. 'Besides,' she added as calmly as she could, 'I can't storm off. I can't swim.'

He laughed aloud at that. 'Again the cool Englishwoman,' he said. 'The brave face, the passionate core. Perhaps I should have spent my time in London instead of New York.'

'Perhaps you should,' said Lora, her heartbeat at last settling down to an almost normal rhythm. 'I'm sure Scotland Yard would have been much less lenient towards your probable activities than the New York police.'

'Perhaps,' said Luc softly. 'But then we would undoubtedly not be here now. And I would not have missed this for the world.' He drew her towards him. Why did her pulse have to leap like that whenever he touched her?

'What are you doing now?' she asked hesitantly, her blood once more thudding through her veins. He grinned at her. 'Giving you your first swimming lesson. What else?'

It was strange, relying so much on a man she ought to loathe, but she found she had no difficulty in letting herself bob on the pool's surface so long as Luc was holding her hand, even if it was only her fingertips, but as soon as he let go her confidence went and she began to sink like a stone once more.

'You have natural talent,' he said later as they sat by the edge, their legs trailing in the cool water. 'All you really lack is confidence. And practice, of course.'

'That depends on how long you're going to keep me prisoner,' said Lora, suddenly unwilling to bring reality flooding back.

Luc gazed at the water for a long moment and then at her. 'As I said, I hope to be able to take you to the airport tomorrow. You will be free to fly away then.'

Lora scrambled up to her feet and ran to get a towel. She was afraid that if she tried to say anything she would choke. How could she have felt so relaxed with a man who was merely using her for his own ends?

He was behind her now, had followed her the few feet to the sun-lounger. 'Lora,' he began.

She buried her face in the towel and, getting a grip on her emotions, spun round to face him. 'What's the matter? Thought I was trying to run away again?'

'I'm beginning to wish I'd never tried to stop you,' he exploded.

'Well, that makes two of us,' she snapped. They glared at each other for a long moment before Lora realised that all she was wearing were her bra and briefs. But she knew it wouldn't have mattered if she had been wearing a suit of armour. Luc was looking at her in a way which made her feel stripped naked. Reddening, she began to wrap the towel around her.

Damn that glint in his eyes. Damn those high cheek-bones and that full, sensuous mouth. And damn him. What right did he have to make her feel so... desirable? She ducked her head to avoid his gaze and began to turn away, but he grasped her wrist and pulled her to him. He looked at her for a long moment and then, as if he had suddenly made his mind up about something, said curtly, 'Get dressed. I am taking you for a drive.'

'Do I have any choice?' she demanded.

He shrugged. 'No. You do not.'

She pulled her wrist free of his grip and stepped back a pace. 'Well, I'll have to go driving in more than a car,' she said stiffly. 'I simply haven't got anything to wear any more. In case it has escaped your notice, Luc, my clothes are at the bottom of your pool.'

He blinked, the merest suspicion of amusement softening his eyes. 'You have a change of clothes in your case, surely?'

'It was an overnight bag,' she informed him. 'I didn't come equipped for a kidnapping.' She pointed at the shapeless pieces of material lying in the pool. 'That was my change of clothes. The ones I was wearing yesterday didn't think much of being hurled out of your Mercedes.'

'What an exciting girl you must be to live with,' mused Luc. 'Most people just send their discarded outfits to some charity. But you seem to find ever new and amusing ways of disposing of yours.'

He glanced down into the pool. 'Not that those ones didn't deserve everything they got. Tell me, are all the clothes you buy as ugly and uncomfortable as that skirt and shirt?'

Lora's eyes sparked. What right did he have to criticise her clothes? 'Why?' she said acidly. 'Do you want to borrow them?'

He reached out and pulled her to him once more. 'I have told you before that I think you are a brave woman,' he said softly. 'But have you not heard of the appalling things that kidnappers do when they grow impatient with their captives?'

'What things?' she gasped, and then, pulling herself together, snapped, 'You wouldn't dare!'

His fingers gently traced the outline of her right ear, her blood heating at the touch. 'What wouldn't I dare?' he said softly.

'I don't know,' breathed Lora. 'Anything. You can seem so cruel, but I can't believe you'd do anything hurtful to me.'

He looked at her for a long moment and then, still gripping her wrist, turned to the house. 'Come with me.'

She tried to struggle but it was no use. He was implacable.

Soon they were in the cool, dim hall of the old, thick-walled house and he was walking purposefully up the stairs. 'I don't want to come with you,' she yelled, grabbing hold of the banister. 'I won't!'

He turned to face her, his black eyes searing into her blue ones. 'What is your imagination telling you that I am going to do to you now, Lora?'

'Nothing,' she lied, trembling.

'Good,' he said silkily. 'Because for once your imagination has got it absolutely right. Now walk up these stairs with me, or I will carry you.'

He let go of her wrist and she rubbed it, staring at him, the tension seeping out of her body as she realised he meant her no harm. 'You went out of your way to scare me just then, didn't you?'

He shrugged slightly. 'Perhaps, yes. You are such an infuriating woman, Lora. You have this quality of inno-cence which seems to protect you completely from re-ality. I know in my heart, and in my head, that making you my captive was the only possible course to solve my predicament. But do you know what you have done?'

Lora looked at him in astonishment. 'What?'

He sighed. 'You have made me feel guilty. I, Luc Jean Henri de la Falaise, made to feel guilty by a maddening girl of twenty-two.'

'Well, don't expect me to feel sorry for you, Luc Jean Henri de la Falaise,' retorted Lora. 'Especially now I know your name. I intend to tell the police everything that has happened.'

'Everything?' asked Luc innocently.

Lora thought of the swimming lesson and how he had kissed her and began to blush. 'You really know how to hit where it hurts,' she said slowly. 'I don't believe a word of what you were saying about feeling rotten over treating me so badly.'

'I said I feel guilty,' snapped Luc. 'Not consumed by remorse. Guilt is not an emotion I am used to, I admit. But whenever I feel it coming over me I start to feel angry too. So you had better watch your step, Lora Seaton. Because your time here is not over yet.'

He turned and continued up the stairs, Lora slowly following. Whatever he said, it was obvious that his conscience was being pricked in more ways than one. Maybe, somehow, she could use that as a lever to make him let her go.

He had disappeared by the time she got to the top of the landing. What was he up to now? Just as she was wondering whether she could make a break for it, a door further up the corridor opened and Luc came out, shepherding before him a tiny, kind-faced woman, her arms piled high with linen.

'Lora,' he called. 'Come. I want to introduce you to someone.' He gazed at her expressionlessly as she joined them. 'This is Maria, the family housekeeper. She is going to find you some clothes you can wear for now.'

He smiled at the woman and then turned back to Lora. 'Any questions?'

'Just a couple,' replied Lora with heavy politeness. 'What on earth is a nice-looking person like this doing working for you? I can't believe a woman like her would have anything to do with a kidnapping.'

'She doesn't,' grated Luc. 'She has been with my family for more years than I care to remember. She is completely loyal to me and can't speak a word of English, so don't waste your breath trying to get her to help you escape.'

'Maybe I'm willing to waste my breath,' challenged Lora. 'Maybe it wouldn't be a waste.'

Luc glanced down at the housekeeper, who was smiling uncertainly at what was obviously an argument but one she didn't understand. He made a remark which cleared her face and she grinned at Lora.

'If by some extraordinary miracle you did manage to tell her your story,' continued Luc, 'she would think you were completely mad.'

Lora glared at him. 'What did you just tell her?'

He gazed at her silently and then made a little impatient gesture with his hands. 'That you were my girlfriend, come to stay for a few days. Why not? She probably saw us in the pool. What more natural explanation could there be?'

Lora felt the blood rush to her face at his words. What more indeed? It was shaming how easily she had supplied Luc with what was nothing more to him than an alibi. 'You trapped me,' she said slowly. 'And you used my emotions to suit yourself.'

His lips twisted. 'Everything is not always as it seems, Lora.'

She swallowed; how could she have been so naïve? So easily overcome by his charm? She was his prisoner, that was the stark truth, and there was no guarantee that she was going to get out of this situation in one piece.

All the fears she had been trying so hard to keep pushed away in a dark recess of her mind rose suddenly and threatened to overwhelm her. Her throat constricted and she could feel tears beginning to prick her eyes. Shaking her head, she made a conscious effort to get a grip on herself. Crying was not going to help the situation.

Luc watched Lora struggle with her conflicting emotions and put a hand on her arm. 'I am not an ogre, Lora. I said I would not hurt you and if you do as I tell you you will come to no harm.'

She clenched her jaw and lifted her head. 'Don't bet on me always obeying your orders, Luc. I will escape from you, I guarantee it.'

He smiled at her. 'I think that very unlikely, if all you insist on wearing is a towel.'

She glared at him. As matter-of-factly as she could, she said, 'No offence to Maria, but we're not exactly similar sizes. What is she going to lend me, an apron?'

His eyes glinted. 'I don't think you need worry on that score. Get what you need from Maria but don't take too long about it. I will expect you downstairs in ten minutes.'

Lora opened her mouth, but before she could say anything he had turned on his heel and was halfway down the stairs. She turned back to Maria with a feeling of unreality. What on earth was she going to be given to wear? The woman seemed to size her up in one lightning glance and then, putting down the linen on an oak chest, turned and beckoned for Lora to follow.

She spoke a few words in French and Lora shook her head. But something in the housekeeper's accent made her try a stab in the dark.

'You're Italian, aren't you?' she breathed, a wild surge of hope flooding through her.

Maria's face split into a grin. '*Sì, sì, sono Italiana.*'

Lora grinned back, filled with such a sense of relief that she suddenly felt quite weak. 'So was my mother,' she replied fluently.

It was not very long before she found herself wearing a cotton dress and a pair of sandals that fitted almost perfectly.

'My daughter's,' explained Maria. 'The dress is a few years old, but that style is so simple it is almost timeless.'

'Your daughter?' said Lora, knowing that from what Luc had said she would have to go carefully if she was to win this woman's confidence.

'She's married now,' went on the housekeeper. She smiled a little sadly. 'Everything changes. And not always for the better.' She sighed and, gripping Lora's hand, led her out of the room. 'Come, Luc will be waiting for you. I'm so glad you're here. Perhaps your presence will lighten the tension in this house.'

'I doubt it,' said Lora grimly.

Maria smiled encouragingly at her. 'Perhaps you can help him in this fight. God knows, he needs all the help he can get.'

'Fight?' said Lora tentatively, but Maria was too busy rattling on to pay her question any attention.

'I can't wait to tell him how wonderful it is to speak Italian to someone else for a change.'

'No!' Lora exclaimed, her heart thudding. She looked at Maria's shocked expression and took a grip on herself. 'I'd rather Luc didn't know. I...' She stopped lamely. She simply could not afford to let him know that she had this one tiny advantage. It presented too good a chance to escape. And Luc had presumably assumed that just because she couldn't speak French she couldn't speak any foreign language.

She took a deep breath and then beamed at Maria. 'Let's keep it our secret for the moment, shall we?' she urged. 'We could have some real fun with him not knowing.' Thankfully Maria, grinning broadly, agreed.

But when Lora made her way downstairs Luc was not waiting for her. She could hear his voice floating down the hall and, as silently as she could, she headed in that direction.

As she got closer she heard her name mentioned and then peered round a half-open door to see Luc in what was obviously his study. He was on the telephone. 'Yes, that is correct,' he said. 'This is the Grand Hotel and I am calling on behalf of Miss Lora Seaton.'

There was silence and then he added, 'She has asked us to tell you that her business in town this morning went well.' Another silence and then, obviously in reply to a question, he added, 'Well, *monsieur*, she sent her apologies but she was offered the chance of an all-day sightseeing trip. She was most insistent I pass on this message. Not at all. Thank you.'

Too late, Lora gathered her scattered wits, pushed the door open further and ran into the room. She grabbed the telephone from Luc and yelled, 'Mark! Mark! I'm here——'

'But, unfortunately, Mark no longer is.' Luc's fingers were pressing down on the telephone cradle and she realised she had acted too late. She was talking to empty air.

He took the receiver from her unresisting hand and replaced it carefully. 'Do you spend a lot of time snooping around people's houses?' he asked conversationally.

'Snooping?' breathed Lora. 'That's rich, coming from you. You're the prize criminal around here. How dare you ring Mark like that and give him a false message from me?'

'It seems perfectly reasonable to me,' replied Luc calmly. 'The last thing I want at the moment is Mr Todd deciding to pop over to France to find out why you have not checked back with him.'

'You——' began Lora.

'I was right in assuming you were expected to ring him after you had been to the *notaire*?' Luc asked calmly.

'What's all this got to do with you?' she demanded. 'Don't you think I might have a right to know something about what's going on?'

'It has everything to do with me,' he replied. 'And as to keeping you informed, that is partly why I am taking you for a drive.'

'Oh.' Geared up for a fight, she felt as though the wind had been taken out of her sails by his newly reasonable attitude. She smoothed her dress awkwardly and was suddenly aware that Luc was surveying her minutely.

'I'm not on offer in some supermarket,' she said, hoping the tartness in her voice would cover the way her heart was thumping. 'Are we really going somewhere, or have you just decided to lock me up in my room like you did last night?'

Luc gazed at her in surprise. 'I did not lock you in your room last night.'

Lora thought of how she had hammered on the door. 'But I heard the key scrape in the lock,' she faltered.

He shook his head. 'No. That would have been the catch. It is very old and inclined to stick.' He reached out a hand to her face and she made herself stare woodenly at him as his fingers brushed her cheek. How could her heart thud like that at his touch when she knew only too well that he was just using her?

'I am sorry if you thought I had locked you in,' he added. 'But it doesn't really matter. I didn't bother too much with safety precautions last night because I did not think that you were in a fit state to escape even if all the doors had been left wide open.'

Lora grasped his fingers and pulled them away. 'It doesn't make any difference,' she said stiffly. 'I was still your prisoner. And am still, for that matter. Why don't you lock me up now and have done with it?'

Luc shrugged, the mockery in his eyes all too apparent. 'Ah, but if I locked you in your room now I would certainly have to come with you to make sure you didn't try some new method of escape and probably kill yourself in the process.'

She glared at him. 'I don't know why I didn't just knot some sheets together last night and climb out of the window.'

Luc took her arm and propelled her towards the car. 'Partly, I suspect, because you were drained of all energy, but mostly because the shutters were only unbarred this morning. In any case, there would be no point in knotting sheets together to escape that room. As I am sure you noticed, it is on the ground floor.'

He opened the door of the Mercedes and motioned her inside. 'Sure you trust me?' said Lora as lightly as she could.

'Why not?' he replied mildly. 'There is nowhere you can escape to.'

'No,' breathed Lora. 'But there is someone I can try to escape from—you.'

Luc's eyes snapped. 'Unless I have your word of honour that you will not try any tricks like the stunt you pulled yesterday, we will go back to the house and stay there until it is time for you to go to the airport.'

'Why should my word mean anything to you?' demanded Lora.

He gazed at her steadily. 'It means a lot to me because I would be prepared to bet it means an awful lot to you. To break your word would put you right down here with the rest of us lesser people.'

'Like kidnappers, you mean,' she flared.

'You know nothing about what I am doing,' said Luc. 'Or why. So how can you sit in judgement?'

'Because I'm your victim,' breathed Lora.

'So you keep reminding me,' he grated. 'But you can rest assured I don't like this any more than you do.'

'You're not about to let me go, though, are you?'

Their eyes met for a long moment and then Luc motioned again for her to get into the car. 'I will not let you go until I get what I want. But I will not harm you and I will free you soon. You will have to be content with that. Now, do I have your word you will not try any tricks?'

'Where are you taking me?' demanded Lora, curiosity overwhelming the last remnants of her ability to remain cool in the face of this man's unbending will.

'Give me your word and get in the car,' said Luc. 'Then you will find out.'

'You can't expect me to give in just like that,' she challenged.

'Why not?' Black eyes met blue and she looked away first.

'Look, Lora,' he said softly, 'it would make no difference to my plans if you decide to do something silly again and ended up in hospital. A broken leg, or whatever else you were foolish enough to achieve, would probably keep you prisoner much more efficiently than I. But then I would have to go to the bother and expense of bringing you fruit and flowers—and there is something about hospitals I find deeply repellent.'

She looked up again, needled by the gentle mockery in his voice. 'Poor you,' she replied scathingly.

'Besides,' he added, pushing a strand of hair away from her face, 'I am not at all certain that I would not be a patient too, in the cardiac-arrest ward.'

She felt a thin flame of heat at his touch and swallowed. 'All right,' she sighed. 'I promise not to try anything silly.'

His eyes softened. 'Don't worry, Lora. I'm not all bad.'

She pulled her seatbelt over her shoulder in an attempt to cover the confusion of emotions that was once more welling in her. 'That is merely your opinion,' she retorted.

His long fingers turned her face towards his. 'And yours too,' he replied.

It was hot in the late afternoon sun, as if all the heat of the day had accumulated, layer upon layer, until it seemed there was no air left, just a thick, gasping blanket which obliterated all thoughts except, How hot it is, all feelings except thirst, all ambitions except the possession of a tall glass of cold water.

'Don't you have air-conditioning in this beast?' said Lora, looking around at the luxury interior of the Mercedes.

'It broke,' replied Luc laconically, and then after a pause added, 'This was my brother's car. He never fixed anything in his life. When something went wrong with one of his many expensive toys he just bought another one.'

'And you get his hand-me-downs?' said Lora, looking quizzically at him. 'Somehow you never struck me as the type to be satisfied with second-best.'

Luc glanced at her sideways. 'Thank you,' he said guardedly.

'So what's your brother driving around in now?' continued Lora.

'He is dead,' said Luc. Silence seemed to envelop them almost as stiflingly as the heat. Lora gazed out of the window feeling more and more out of her depth with this man with every mile they drove. What did he want with her?

And then, as they swept round a bend, all thoughts of her predicament temporarily evaporated. 'Oh,' she breathed. 'Oh, look—the château.'

Luc gave it no more than the flicker of a glance but his face tightened perceptibly as he did so.

'It's the same château I was trying to make for this afternoon,' Lora said. And then, snapping her thoughts to the present, she stared at Luc. 'Isn't it?'

Almost as if it was against his will Luc slowed the car as they passed the château's huge wrought-iron gates.

A long, weed-specked drive led up to the once lovely building. Now that Lora was closer she could see roof slates missing and huge brown bruises on the walls where the stucco had fallen away. 'I could be there now if it hadn't been for you,' she said slowly, turning back to Luc. 'I could be free.'

'No,' he said flatly. 'You would not be free. No one lives there. It is empty. Boarded up.'

'Who owns it?' asked Lora. 'Don't tell me you do. It wouldn't surprise me in the least—you seem to own everything else around here.'

There was no reply as she twisted around in her seat to catch a last glimpse of white through the trees, which were so heavy in leaf, they looked almost black in the blazing sun. When she turned back she was shocked at the taut expression on Luc's face. He looked as though he had been carved from stone. 'Luc?' she said tentatively.

'The château is nothing to do with me,' he replied at last. 'It is owned by strangers.'

Lora slowly sat back in her seat and said nothing until, a few miles later, he pulled up by a grass verge. He turned the ignition key and sat silent for a while, almost as if he was listening to the engine ticking as it cooled in the still air.

Then he glanced at Lora and smiled. 'Still here? I know you gave me your word but I'm surprised you haven't made at least one attempt to throw yourself out of the car.'

Lora's eyes narrowed. 'What were you going to do?' she enquired icily. 'Give me fifty yards' start?'

Luc sighed. 'I am sorry. That was unfair. But you are free to get out, if you wish.'

'Thank you so much,' she grated, making a grab for the door-handle. But Luc's hand was over hers before she had properly gripped it. Slowly he lifted her hand to his lips and kissed her palm. 'You are so thorny, Lora.'

'Prickly,' she corrected, snapping the word out to cover her own confusion. She tried to withdraw her hand but he held it fast.

'I prefer thorny,' he said. 'It reminds me of roses. And yet they have such soft velvet petals.' He lifted a gentle finger to her face. 'Like your lips.'

Lora could feel the blood thundering in her ears at his touch. 'Don't be so silly.' She swallowed but knew that, whatever she said, she did not want to move away.

'Is it so silly to say you are like a rose, an English rose?'

'Yes, absolutely,' she forced out, unable to wrest her gaze from his eyes and wondering what would happen if she allowed herself to be taken in by those deceptively soft black depths.

'Why did your parents call you Lora?' he said at last, the tension in the air surrounding them easing fractionally. It was such a simple question, after all the loaded meaning in his look and touch, that she was caught off guard.

'Wh-what?' she faltered, and then lied quickly, 'No particular reason.'

His eyebrows arched. 'Really? I thought you were a very English-sounding *Laura*—L.A.U.R.A.—until I looked at your passport and discovered that you are really something quite different. I must admit I found it intriguing. Why not spell your name the traditional way?'

'Oh, my father didn't like conventional names,' said Lora, thinking, with a sudden shaft of sadness, of her parents. When would she ever see them again?

'It suits you,' said Luc. 'I should imagine you are not a conventional daughter.'

'Conventional?' said Lora. 'You don't know my parents.'

'I should like to meet them,' Luc replied.

Lora shrugged. 'Difficult,' she said shortly, trying to smile but failing miserably. 'They spend at least six months of the year travelling the world. They could be anywhere from Brisbane to Botswana.'

Luc's fingers took hold of hers and held them steady. 'I'm sorry,' he said. 'You obviously miss your parents very much.'

'It's silly,' she said unsteadily. 'But I do miss them sometimes. Especially now. As soon as I left school and went to college they decided to up sticks and see the world. I never know where I'm going to get a postcard from next. Quite exciting, I suppose.'

He looked at her in a puzzled fashion. 'You went to college when you left school?'

'Yes,' said Lora and then, realising his puzzlement, explained, 'It was a different one from the secretarial place.' She gulped. All these memories, just when she didn't want them.

'What sort of college?' he probed.

'Art,' she replied, adding abruptly, 'But I left before the course finished.'

CHAPTER FOUR

'WHAT happened? Didn't the course agree with you?' Luc asked.

'It wasn't the art,' she began. 'It was... Oh, never mind.'

'A love-affair?' he supplied.

'If you must know, yes,' she replied at last. 'It just didn't work out.'

'He was a lecturer?' asked Luc.

She nodded. 'I felt so serious about him, but it meant absolutely nothing as far as he was concerned. Then I found he was notorious for having affairs with his students and I felt so humiliated I just had to get away.'

She sighed. 'I went for a long holiday with my parents and when I came back I decided to sign up for the secretarial course. I couldn't bear going back to the art college. And secretarial qualifications are always useful, so I was told. So I decided to stick with it, no matter what.'

'No wonder you were so proud of yourself,' said Luc softly. 'But it seems a shame to have shut the door on your artistic talents.'

'Oh, well,' she shrugged. 'Maybe one day I'll get the chance to take up painting again.'

'I'm sure you will,' he said gently. His kindness was more difficult to bear than his mockery and before she could help herself she sniffed. What on earth was the matter with her? Why on earth did she suddenly feel like crying over a long-dead affair and a lost opportunity?

She sniffed again, and then looked quickly at Luc. 'I've got a cold,' she said untruthfully.

He reached into a pocket and pulled out a large white handkerchief. 'Here.'

Blindly she took it and blew her nose loudly. She peered over the folds of white linen to see that he was gazing at her with compassion tinged with some amusement.

'What's the matter?' she demanded.

He smiled. 'Nothing.'

'Tell me,' she insisted.

He looked at her again and shrugged. 'Nothing. Really. Just...'

'What?' she repeated.

'Just the way you blow your nose,' he said at last. 'As if your life depended on it.'

'Unlike French girls, I suppose, who dab delicately at their immaculately made-up faces,' retorted Lora fiercely, feeling suddenly terribly exposed over such a triviality.

He grasped her hand again. 'Lora, I did not bring you here to laugh at you. Really.' He paused and then added earnestly, 'I like the way you blow your nose.'

Lora giggled in spite of herself. 'Oh, I'm glad about that,' she gasped, halfway between tears and hiccups. 'I'll keep your hankie as a memento of a kidnapper's tolerance.'

He glanced sideways at her. 'You can use it as a white flag when you finally decide to let down your defences.'

Her fingers tightened around the thin material. 'You are my kidnapper, Luc, and I am your prisoner,' she said in a low voice. 'You keep making me forget that,

but it doesn't change what you've done. I can't afford
to let down my defences with you.'

He looked at her. 'But you already have, *chérie*,' he
replied gently. 'You just keep putting them back up
again. One day you'll get rid of them completely and I
intend to be there. It will be a revelation.'

'Don't hold your breath,' snapped Lora, unbalanced
by his cool assurance and determined to change the
subject. 'Where are you taking me today? Some new
gaol where the police won't find you?'

If she expected to rattle him, she failed. 'Why should
the police be looking for me?' he shrugged. 'I am a well-
respected citizen of this community.'

She opened her mouth, but no words came out. At
this moment it was obvious that Luc held all the aces.
He watched her expression change from defiance to one
of set stubbornness and sighed. Then, gesturing at the
surrounding countryside, he said, 'This is where I wanted
to bring you today, Lora. I wanted to show you
something.'

She looked around in some confusion at the rolling
landscape. 'What? I can't see anything.'

He gazed at her curiously. 'Do you not know where
you are? Can you not guess?'

'No,' she snapped. 'I can't. Where are we?'

But instead of answering her he looked around at the
gentle slopes covered in grape-vines, the rose bushes at
the end of each row in full bloom. 'It is not spectacular
scenery,' he said softly. 'But to me it is very beautiful.'

Lora said nothing. She was simply not going to
humour him.

But he was not the kind of man to be fazed by frozen
conversations. He put his hand gently under her chin

and forced her to face him. 'Don't you think it is beautiful here, Lora?'

'What does it matter what I think?' she blurted out.

'It matters a great deal,' he said seriously. 'And I should like to know your opinion.'

'This is silly,' she quavered. 'It's just countryside, like everywhere else around here.'

'True, I suppose,' he shrugged. 'But take a good look all the same and tell me what you think.'

Lora glanced around at the ordered greenness of the landscape, at the rich brown earth, the deep blue sky. They had stopped in a small valley and through a gap in the hills she could see more greenness fading away into the hot haziness of the horizon. There was something about its ordered simplicity and lushness that was very charming.

'It is beautiful,' she said in a low voice. 'Like a Cézanne painting, almost. But I don't know why you think I should recognise this place.'

'The contract you were to have signed today was for this valley,' replied Luc. 'For almost as far as you can see, in fact. And that includes the château you seemed so fond of.'

Lora blinked. 'The contract was for a golf course, Luc. That's what Mark told me.'

Luc nodded. 'And in this instance he told you the truth. If you had signed that contract this morning all these vines would have been grubbed up and this whole area would have been turned into a golf course, traipsed over by foolish tourists paying exorbitant prices for their pleasure.'

'Tourism means money,' said Lora. 'I expect the area could do with a big injection of cash. All those visitors buying everything from postcards to...' She paused and added defiantly, 'To your precious French wine.'

Luc stared at her grimly. 'In this deal most of the money will be going to your precious Mr Todd.'

'You're being silly,' began Lora.

Luc gripped her wrist and pulled her to him. 'Am I?' he grated. 'Mark Todd doesn't do anything unless there's a big fat profit in it for him. The building will probably be done on the cheap and after a brief honeymoon period he will no doubt disappear, leaving a lot of debts behind him.'

Lora tried to shake herself free but his grip was like a vice. 'I don't believe you,' she cried. 'You're blowing this up out of all proportion.'

His face was only a few inches from her own. She looked into his eyes and felt herself falling into their black inkiness. She tried to look away but she knew she was losing control. 'Why should I exaggerate?' he said softly.

'Because you're jealous,' she replied hotly. 'Jealous that Mark's got what you want.'

His eyes travelled down her face and she could feel it flame under his gaze. As if he were setting a match to her feelings. As if he knew they were just under the surface waiting to surge into a passion which she knew she had to hold back.

'Does Mark Todd own you too?' rasped Luc.

Lora's stomach gave a sickening twist at the thought of what had happened last time she had seen Mark and then gave herself a little mental shake. It was Luc she had to contend with now. Luc and the almost impossible situation he had thrust her into.

She stared boldly at him. 'Of course Mark and I are lovers,' she lied. 'We——'

But before she could continue he had pulled her to him, his lips on hers, his tongue tasting the soft, sweet moisture within. Fury erupted within her and then died as a hotter flame ran through her veins. She wanted this man. Wanted him as much as he wanted her and though her voice could lie her body could not. His mouth became more insistent, his fingers stroking through her hair and then down her back, effortlessly unzipping her dress and drawing a line of fire down her spine.

Without even knowing it her free hand crept around his neck, her fingers rubbing the crisp, short hairs at the nape. It was no use. She couldn't fight him any more, and she simply didn't want to.

He stopped for one burning moment while his eyes consumed her and then he eased the strap of her dress over her shoulder.

'No,' she whispered, and his fingers stopped.

'Truly?' he said.

'No, not truly,' she sighed. And as he bent his head to kiss the base of her throat she knew that she could never say no to this man.

'Oh, Luc,' she gasped, her voice no more than a ragged sigh.

He drew back slowly and caressed her cheek. 'Does Mark do this to you?'

Lora stared at him uncomprehendingly. 'Mark?' she echoed.

'Your lover,' said Luc. 'You know, the property tycoon I'm so jealous of.' His voice was husky and she could see a muscle thudding in his cheek.

'You didn't mean any of what you just did,' said Lora slowly, feeling a cold wave of sickness wash over her.

'Should I have done?' he said grimly.

Lora ignored the question. 'It was just a game to you,' she said slowly. 'A game. You just wanted to score a point off another man.'

Luc sat back and gazed at her. But she could have sworn that he was not really seeing her. It was as though he was examining his own soul. 'Perhaps it was a game at first,' he admitted at last. 'But the more I desire you, the more I realise I cannot get back at Mark through you. This is turning out to be a more difficult game to play than I expected, Lora. You have an extraordinary effect on me, and I'm not sure it's one that I like.'

He eased the strap of her dress back over her shoulder and pulled up her zip as casually as if he were dressing himself. 'You are like forbidden fruit. I keep telling myself that I cannot taste, that it is not right.' He smiled wryly. 'But I do not always do what I am told.'

Lora glared at him, her cheeks hot with anger. 'You are still holding my wrist. And your grip is too tight,' she forced out through clenched teeth.

He lifted her hand to his face and kissed the inside of her wrist. 'I am sorry,' he said seriously. 'It was wrong of me to have taken advantage of your vulnerability. I have not behaved at all like . . .' He paused, and then added with a tiny ironic inflexion, 'An English gentleman.'

She clasped her wrist where he had held it, staring all the time at his eyes. There was a moment's silence. And then, very deliberately, she slapped his cheek as hard as she could.

'That is because, for once, you and I are in complete agreement,' she retorted.

Her hand dropped and she glared at him, daring him to retaliate. Instead his fingers briefly touched the reddening marks on his cheek and then he bent his head and smiled. 'You don't pull your punches, do you?'

Lora swallowed. Before this trip she had never hit anyone in her life and now she had slapped Luc twice. He was not the sort of person anyone but a maniac would consider trying to beat up. 'No, I don't suppose I do,' she agreed slowly.

He smiled at her and she felt her heart give a double thud. 'Do you believe me when I say I am sorry?' he said gently.

'Do you mean it?' she asked, astonished by his line of sudden seeming humility.

Luc shrugged. 'I am sorry if I upset you, yes. But if you mean am I sorry I kissed you, then the answer has to be no.'

'You did more than just kiss me,' Lora said hotly. 'You——'

'Took advantage of you?' supplied Luc. 'Yes. I did. But do you know something?' He turned to look at her as he started the engine.

'What?' she said guardedly.

'I enjoyed it every bit as much as I believe you did.'

Lora glared at him. 'Do you know just exactly what you are?' she said fiercely.

'Yes,' he replied equably. 'And I can say it in fourteen different languages.'

'Only fourteen?' Lora retorted. 'You surprise me.'

'You must make allowances for me,' he said. 'I only managed to get halfway around the world before I had to return home.'

'You mean somebody actually wanted you back?' she asked in mock-amazement. 'How extraordinary.'

There was silence and then he said, 'I came home because my father and brother died in a car crash.'

Lora's jaw dropped. 'Oh,' she gasped. There was silence and then in a small voice she added, 'I'm sorry.'

He glanced at her and his eyes softened. 'Sympathy for me, Lora? This will never do. You can't start thinking of me as a human being. After all, where would it lead?'

'Don't you ever let down your guard?' she asked.

'Not to people I kidnap, no.'

She gazed at his strong profile; his skin was bronze in the setting sun. 'I shouldn't think you've ever kidnapped anyone in your life before,' she said softly.

'And what makes you think that, Miss Secretary Seaton?'

'Because you're forceful enough to get your own way ninety-nine times out of a hundred.'

He smiled at her. 'So if my kidnapping you is a last resort, don't you think you should be a bit more careful of what you say to me?'

Lora gazed steadily at him. 'I suppose I should,' she agreed. 'But then I am the most completely tactless person I know. I can't seem to help myself.'

'I had noticed,' he said drily. 'But please don't stop. I find your remarks about how I will cope with prison life rather entertaining.'

Lora stared out of the window as they pulled away from the verge. Her exterior was one of pretended indifference, but inside her emotions were seething. Did

Luc have any idea of the effect he was having on her? Just one look from him was enough to make her forget the whole mess he had got her into. And if she spent any longer in his company he would send her up in flames.

'I want to go back to my room,' she said at last.

'Back to the house of your hateful kidnapper?' said Luc in mock-surprise.

'You can lock me in my bedroom,' flashed Lora. 'And then at least I can be away from you.'

'Then it seems I must apologise again,' said Luc gravely.

'Why?' demanded Lora.

'Because I have decided to take you out to dinner. And so it seems you will have the ordeal of my company for a little longer yet.'

'You're crazy,' breathed Lora. 'Haven't you thought of the fact that I might just try to escape?'

'You can try,' said Luc. 'But if you go before dinner you will miss a wonderful meal, and if you attempt anything afterwards you will probably be too full to move.'

'Perhaps I like the idea of freedom more than food,' replied Lora defiantly.

'Impossible,' mocked Luc. 'You cannot be serious.'

'You certainly never seem to be,' observed Lora hotly.

The Mercedes crunched to a halt outside a lovely old *auberge*. It was set in the countryside as though it had grown there and, although there were a few other cars parked near by, it was obviously in the middle of nowhere.

Luc gestured at the surrounding fields. 'You do not stand a chance of escaping to anywhere from here,' he said. 'Why not just accept that you will have to be my guest for a little longer?'

Lora took another look around the landscape. He was right—she could not get very far away from this place. 'Well, I suppose it seems I have no choice,' she admitted grudgingly.

He held his hand out and, wonderingly, Lora took it. 'I admire you very much, you know,' he told her. 'We are both bound in a situation we don't much like. Shall we declare a truce?'

His hand closed around hers and Lora found herself returning his firm grip. 'You can have a temporary cease-fire, if you like, Luc. But I warn you, as soon as I see a chance to escape I shall take it.'

He nodded. 'Done. There is no way you will ever escape from me, but I shall enjoy watching your future attempts as much as I have the last few.'

Lora's eyes sparked. But before she could say anything he lifted his hands in mock-alarm. 'OK, I get your drift. Let's eat.'

'You should watch out, you know,' she told him as they walked to the restaurant door. 'I might stab you with my steak knife.'

Luc smiled. 'I will try to ensure that you are only given a spoon tonight,' he replied.

The restaurant was small, dark, and as they entered Lora began to feel her neck prickling at the idea of spending the evening in such close contact with Luc. The atmosphere was too intimate, too seductive. She glanced at one of the many secluded tables where a couple were so engrossed in each other, it was obvious that they wouldn't notice if sawdust was put in front of them.

She felt her mouth go dry as they were led to an equally secluded table.

Luc broke off an enthusiastic conversation with the head waiter and turned to her. 'What would you like to eat, Lora?'

'Sawdust,' she said unthinkingly, and then, as his lips twitched in amused surprise, she couldn't stop herself from smiling back.

'With a side-order of wood shavings?' he asked mock-seriously.

Lora looked at his handsome face and the way he was smiling at her and, with a great effort of will, closed her eyes. This was no good. He was just too damn charming. She had to keep her distance, or she would be swallowed whole—and then probably spat out, she thought bitterly. If nothing else, the earlier events of the afternoon should serve as a warning.

She buried herself in the gigantic menu and jumped as though she had been given an electric shock when his hand pulled it away from her face.

'You can't hide from me, Lora,' he said, staring intently at her.

'I was looking at the menu,' she said stiffly and unconvincingly.

Amusement glittered in his eyes. 'Ah, yes, of course—the great French expert.'

Lora glared at him. 'That's not fair.'

Luc shrugged. 'It was a joke. That's all. Or don't you have such things in England?'

'Yes,' she flared. 'But they're mostly in English.' It was childish and she knew it, but somehow she just couldn't stop herself.

Luc picked up his fork and examined it in minute detail. 'If you stay here long enough you will end up speaking French as well as I.'

Lora's heart missed a beat. 'You said I could go back tomorrow.'

He put his fork back down on the table and grasped one of her hands. 'Things might take longer than I hoped, Lora. But you will be home as soon as possible.'

She wrenched her hand away and pushed her chair back so suddenly that it screeched on the polished wood floor. 'What?' she demanded.

'I said,' repeated Luc, 'that things are going to take a little longer. I made a few phone calls this afternoon and my plans are going more slowly than I hoped.'

'You rat!' she yelled, oblivious of the other diners. 'How dare you do this to me?'

Luc sat calmly in his chair, only his eyes betraying the intensity of his feelings. Lora could feel his gaze holding her like a magnetic beam.

He sighed. 'I dare because I have to.'

'You don't have to at all. You could let me go right now. You're a rich man. What's a lousy golf course to you?'

Luc's hands gripped the arms of his chair so tightly that Lora could see his knuckles shine white in the dim light of the restaurant. 'More than you will probably ever know,' he said. 'Now sit down.'

For an instant that seemed to last as long as eternity they stared at each other and then Lora's eyes dropped and she sat down. It was as though the whole restaurant breathed a sigh of relief.

A waiter picked up her menu, which had fallen to the floor, and Lora scanned it blindly. Luc seemed engrossed in the wine list but she knew that he was conscious of every move she was making.

Carefully she laid the menu on the table and leant across to him. His eyes met hers and she swallowed, but she was not going to back down. 'I don't care how important this deal is to you. Because in the end that's all it is. A deal. Money in the bank. And I'm more important than cold cash.'

'Lora——' he began, but she swept on.

'I want my freedom, Luc Jean Henri de la Falaise. And I'm going to fight you every inch of the way to get it. Right now there's nothing I can do. As you say, we're in the middle of nowhere and you have my money, passport and ticket. But if you think I'm going just to sit around tamely for days on end and wait for you to release me, well, you've got another think coming.'

Luc stared at her for a moment and then poured out the wine the waiter had brought and raised his glass to her. 'To you, Lora. I salute your courage, but let us not forget that we have agreed a temporary cease-fire.'

Lora breathed deeply. 'You don't take anything I've said at all seriously, do you?'

He held his glass up to the light and squinted at it critically. 'Not a bad colour, and the taste is good for such a young wine.'

'Luc!' She felt like taking her shoe off and banging it on the table to get his attention. He had to be the most infuriating man she'd ever met.

He looked at her. 'As you say, Lora, I have your money, passport and ticket. You do not speak French. Therefore I have the upper hand. But I do take one thing seriously.'

'What?' she demanded.

'You,' he said softly.

Lora's lips parted incredulously. 'As a hostage or as a woman?' she said tightly, her heart hammering.

His eyes roamed lazily over her face and she could feel herself reddening under his gaze.

'The waiter is waiting,' he said gently. 'What would you like to eat?' He paused and then asked, 'Would you like me to order for you? The menu is all in French.'

Lora glared at him. 'There are such things as French restaurants in England, you know. I'm not totally helpless.'

Luc shrugged. 'As you like.'

Seething with a whole sea of conflicting emotions, Lora turned to the menu and realised in dismay that Luc had been absolutely right. She couldn't tell what anything was. In desperation she pointed randomly at what she hoped was a starter and a main course and sat back as Luc ordered efficiently for himself.

He was smiling at her again, damn him. 'Looking forward to your meal?' he enquired.

'I didn't know how to pronounce it,' she admitted grimly, 'and I certainly don't know what it is, but I just hope you've forgotten all your money and have to wash the dishes for three months to pay for it.'

'Unlikcly,' he replied blandly. 'They installed an electric dishwasher here just two weeks ago.'

'Why are you smiling like that?' demanded Lora. 'You look like the cat that's got the cream. What's the joke?'

Luc shrugged. 'No joke. Let's just say that this evening I have cause to celebrate.'

'I don't see why,' she remarked. 'I thought things were going badly for you.'

Luc gazed at her speculatively. 'I said they were going more slowly than I expected. I did not say they were going badly. On the contrary, everything is going very well.'

'Why?' she demanded. 'What has today changed?'

'My life,' Luc said simply. He poured some more wine into Lora's glass and lifted his again to hers.

'To you,' he said softly. 'Thank you, Lora Seaton.'

'To me?' answered Lora incredulously. 'What have I done?'

'Been my captive,' said Luc. 'Not a particularly pleasant role, although I have done my best to lighten it for you.'

'Thank you so much,' replied Lora with heavy irony. 'But I still don't understand.'

Luc sighed. 'You were supposed to sign a property contract this morning. When you did not appear at the specified time the deal that Mark Todd hoped to pull off became null and void.'

Lora shrugged. 'There is nothing to stop him re-negotiating.'

Luc put his glass down. 'Just one thing,' he said. 'Me.'

She opened her mouth to question him further but was stopped by the return of the waiter. What looked like a pale grey sausage on a plate was put in front of her. She stared at it in disbelief. 'What's this?' she said incredulously.

Luc seemed to be busy squeezing a wedge of lemon over his smoked salmon, but Lora caught the amusement in his eyes as he stared with a mask of polite interest at her plate.

'*Andouillette*,' he said innocently. 'It is a peasant dish. Quite delicious here, so I am told, although I do not care for it myself.'

Lora poked the sausage gingerly with her knife and what seemed like a collection of small watch-springs popped out. She leapt back as if she had been bitten and stared horrified at Luc.

'You're laughing at my dinner,' she said incredulously.

Luc shook his head, his eyes sparkling with amusement. 'No, *chérie*, I am laughing at you. You look like a débutante who has just been handed a slug at a cocktail party.'

Lora's eyes widened at his words. 'It isn't...?'

He grinned. 'A special kind of slug? No. We might eat snails, but there are things even we draw the line at. No, Lora, *andouillette* is a sort of sausage stuffed with tripes and things from the insides of animals.' He shrugged. 'I am sorry; my English does not really extend to recipes. Although...' His lips twitched and Lora looked at him suspiciously.

'Although what?' she demanded.

Luc squeezed a little more lemon over his salmon and took a bite. 'Mmm, this is quite delicious.'

'Luc! I swear I'll scream if you don't tell me what you were going to say.'

He smiled at her. 'It was simply that I believe what you have ordered for the main course is a speciality of the house. Henri, the *patron*, was very pleased at your choices. He said you must be very chic, very informed.'

'What did I order, Luc?' grated Lora.

He ate some more salmon and then smiled wickedly at her. 'Stuffed pigs' feet.'

She pushed her plate away as far as it could go and then stared at Luc in mute appeal.

'Not hungry after all?' he asked.

'I'm starving,' she hissed. 'And you know it. What are you having for the main course?'

'Steak,' he said succinctly. 'Henri does it very well, and it reminds me of the nicer aspects of New York.'

'Steak?' Lora almost wailed. 'You can't do this to me, Luc. You can't honestly say that you are going to sit there and eat steak while I'm handed a plate of pigs' trotters.'

He shrugged. 'You did insist on ordering for yourself and——'

'You know very well why I insisted,' she interrupted furiously. 'Because you were making fun of me. I can't believe you let me order this stuff.'

Luc stared at her incredulously. 'Let you?' he repeated. 'You would have attacked me with your cake fork if I had had the bad sense even to point out that you were holding your menu upside-down.'

'I was what?' breathed Lora.

His eyes wide with innocence, he looked her straight in the face. 'I thought perhaps it might be some new swanky fashion in England. You know—I am so well-educated I can even read menus the wrong way around. Tell me——' Luc leaned forward '—do you read them back to front, too?'

Lora glared at him. 'I was not holding the menu upside-down, Luc, and you know it.'

He sat back with his hands outstretched and an innocent expression on his face. 'All right, I admit it. It was a childish joke on my part—but I nearly had you believing it.' Then, smiling, he added, 'You should have seen your face when the waiter arrived with your *andouillette*. That I would not have missed for all the ransom money in the world.'

Lora took a piece of French bread and began to butter it savagely. 'You are the most impossible man I've ever met,' she bit out.

He raised an eyebrow. 'You are not a very possible person yourself. I have always thought that women were a most extraordinary race of individuals, but you . . .' He paused as if lost for words. 'You, Lora, have to be awarded the biscuit.'

His gaze caught hers and Lora could feel her fury draining away like water down a plug-hole. She gave Luc a small smile. 'In that case, Luc, do you think you could award it to me now? Even a biscuit would be better than pigs' trotters.'

CHAPTER FIVE

THE meal was over and Lora was full of steak and a growing goodwill towards Luc that she was trying hard, but without a hundred per cent success, to hide.

'It was good of you to swap meals with me,' she said at last, feeling awkward at the necessity of thanking him.

He shook his head slightly. 'If it had been any other restaurant I would have simply told you to order again, but I have known Henri since I was a child and he is proud of his local specialities.'

'And so you didn't want to hurt his feelings,' said Lora softly.

Luc stood up suddenly. 'It would be bad for business to alienate local tradespeople. Especially such an influential man as Henri.'

'Of course,' said Lora blandly, watching Henri hurry up to say goodbye. It was obvious that there was no way Luc was going to admit that friendship was his main motivation here. 'I'd like to be friends with you,' she said under her breath as she gazed at Luc's back, and was suddenly shocked by the depth of affection she felt for this man.

Desire was one thing. It could be explained away as some sort of primeval instinct which couldn't be denied but had to be controlled. Affection, on the other hand, was a plant that surely had to be nurtured. And it seemed to be growing up without any encouragement at all between her and Luc. She thought of his amusement at her reaction to the *andouillette* and smiled a little bitterly. If she could not afford to desire this man, then friendship and affection had to be out of the question. They were not the sort of emotions you were supposed to feel towards someone who had just kidnapped you. The one thing she had to do was get away from him, just as fast as she could.

The stars were diamonds on black velvet as they drove home. Lora gazed at Luc's profile as he concentrated on the road ahead and then said, 'Why did you do that?'

'Do what?' he asked, not turning his head.

'Take me out to dinner and swap meals with me. It's not exactly normal behaviour for a kidnapper.'

He smiled suddenly. 'You seem to know an awful lot about what normal kidnappers do and don't do. Have you got a handbook on the etiquette of kidnapping? Or do you set yourself up as a victim so you can go round as some sort of inspector, awarding us all stars for threatening behaviour, quality of blindfolds, legibility of ransom notes, and so forth?'

'You know precisely what I meant,' said Lora. 'And I don't find what you're saying that funny. You've taken away my freedom, remember? And this whole situation is so weird. You tell me you've kidnapped me, but you don't want a ransom. You tell me you're not going to let me go and then you take me out to dinner. Just what exactly is going on?'

Luc sighed. 'As I told you in the restaurant, Lora, the whole point of keeping you out of circulation was so that you wouldn't sign that contract Mark Todd is banking on. If Mark had come himself I wouldn't have thought twice about having him thrown in a dark cellar for a couple of days. And Carole...'

Something in his voice made Lora look at him in surprise. 'You know Carole?' she questioned.

'Well enough to bribe her.'

Lora stared at him, thunderstruck. 'You bribed Carole?' she repeated slowly.

'Yes, why not?' he asked. 'Does it shock you?'

Lora thought of Carole and her hard-faced cheerfulness, and gestured helplessly. 'No. I suppose it doesn't,' she admitted. 'So that's why she had flu so badly that she couldn't go on the trip.'

'Yes,' agreed Luc sardonically. 'It was a very expensive illness indeed. And when she told me you were going instead I almost felt like asking for my money back. And then when I saw you...' He stopped again.

'You thought I was some sort of assistant,' Lora remembered.

'I saw you long before you saw me,' he said. 'I tailed you all the way from Mark's office in London.'

'You did what?' Were there no limits to which this man would not go?

'I was on the same plane, and in the taxi behind yours from the airport to the hotel.' There was a pause as he slowed to negotiate a sharp bend and then he continued, 'You had an argument with the taxi driver. Amusing, really, since neither of you had the slightest idea what the other was talking about.'

Lora thought back to that afternoon. Was it really only the day before? 'He hadn't charged me enough,' she remembered. 'And it wasn't until the hotel manager came to my rescue that we got it all sorted out. The taxi driver was amazed.'

'I'm not surprised,' said Luc drily. 'So was I. In fact I was so surprised that I thought Carole had got it completely wrong and that there would be some grim-faced woman in enormous shoulder-pads coming along any minute to take charge of you.'

'Thank you very much,' retorted Lora.

He looked sideways at her. 'Not at all. It was quite obvious from that little episode that bribery was not going to work in your case. So I took a desperate measure. Not one I would normally even contemplate. I kidnapped you.'

'Well, you've gone too far,' said Lora. 'What are you going to do if I tell you the first thing I'm going to do when you set me free is go to the police?'

'Have you considered that I might not set you free?' Luc asked, his voice dangerously quiet.

Lora gulped. 'I...' she began.

'Well, think about it now,' he said softly.

She swallowed once more and lifted her chin. 'Why don't you just kill me now and have done with it?' she said, trying to control the quaver in her voice. 'It's nice and quiet here. You could dump me in one of those fields.' She stared at him, daring him to stop the car and attack her.

The car screeched to a halt and Luc turned to face her, furious. 'Why don't you just leap out when I'm going really fast and save me the trouble?' he snarled.

She glared back. 'Why should I do your dirty work for you?'

His eyes were snapping with anger. 'Why not? You've practically just given me step-by-step instructions on how to dispose of you. Don't tell me——' he slapped his forehead in mock-enlightenment '—I know, you've got a book on handy tips for murderers, right?'

'You're being ridiculous,' she quavered.

His eyebrows came down in one straight line as he scowled at her. 'Somebody in this car is being ridiculous, and it is not me.'

'You were the one who threatened me with never being able to go home,' she replied hotly.

He closed his eyes and sighed impatiently. 'I said you should think about it. As I've said before, you have this quality of innocence about you which seems to believe that no one is ever going to hurt you.'

'Well, no one ever does, really,' said Lora.

He looked at her in exasperation. 'If I were a normal kidnapper, whatever that means, how do you think I would react if you told me you were going straight to the police?'

Lora shrugged. 'I don't care,' she said. 'You're not a normal kidnapper and I know you're not going to hurt me.'

He thrust his face very close to hers. 'You are not doing a very good job for my male ego, Miss Seaton. Don't I scare you at all?'

She smiled nervously at him. 'Actually, you terrify the life out of me sometimes.'

He breathed deeply. 'Good. Now let's go home.'

Lora tried hard to remember some reference points on the way back to the house. If she was to escape she had to know something of the surrounding countryside; but it was no use. The roads they used were small lanes and, even with the moonlight flooding the vineyards, everywhere looked the same.

Soon the big car had crunched up the gravel drive to the old farmhouse and she looked at the building with a weary sigh.

'It's not that bad,' said Luc.

She glared at him. 'How would you know?' she snapped. 'You're not the one who's being kept under lock and key.'

There was silence then and she twisted her hands in her lap. 'I could have stood on that table in the restaurant tonight and screamed blue murder. Someone would have intervened. I could be free by now.'

'Everybody in that restaurant knows me,' said Luc. 'I'm a pillar of the local community, remember? You could have stood on that table and screamed any colour of murder you liked and all I would have needed to do would be to say you were suffering from hysteria or hallucinations and had forgotten your tranquillisers.'

Lora conjured up the scene in her mind and realised the horrible reality of what he had said. 'You took a hell of a gamble,' she whispered.

'And I won,' he replied calmly. 'But then it was not much of a gamble. As we have already agreed, I have all the aces.'

Lora stared at his face, his strong features thrown into sharp contrast by the moonlight. 'Well, I'll just have to be the joker in the pack,' she retorted with false bravado, before fumbling for the door-handle.

She stumbled out of the car with numb desperation. It had all seemed so unreal at first, the way Luc had spirited her away. Somehow the sunshine had made it seem a game. She thought of the swimming lesson he had given her. How he had stopped her from drowning. Had all of that meant nothing to him? And if she had meant nothing to him, why had he gone to all the risk of taking her out? The more questions she asked herself, the more confused she became. But one look at Luc's grim expression made her know better than to start asking him anything more tonight. Besides, she didn't know whether she wanted to hear the answers.

His expression softened as he took in her woebegone face. 'You are tired,' he said softly.

'A little,' she admitted, not daring to trust herself to more words.

'Come.' He put his arm around her and guided her up the steps. The contact of his body was disturbing to say the least, and Lora was glad when they reached the door and he let go of her to use his keys. She was beginning to feel that she simply couldn't cope with her emotions any longer.

He shrugged off his jacket almost as soon as he was in the hall, and threw it over the banisters. 'I need to talk to you, Lora,' he said. 'Come and have a drink with me before you go to bed.'

She stood irresolute, like a startled deer. 'Is that a request or a command?' she said at last.

He raked his fingers through his hair. The black crispness of it stood up unevenly and Lora suppressed a desire to reach up and smooth it down. 'I'm not going to force you,' he said patiently, 'but I think a talk would be useful for both of us. I have a proposition to make to you.'

Lora shrugged helplessly and let him shepherd her into the long, low sitting-room. It was plain but comfortable, with the light from several lamps picking out the soft deep colours of the rugs on the terracotta tiled floor. There was a huge fireplace to give warmth on winter nights, but no flames danced in it tonight. It was simply too hot, even at midnight.

She sat down limply in a low armchair and watched Luc stride to the drinks tray. 'Whisky?' he asked and she nodded, reflecting that she would probably have nodded if he had suggested arsenic and tonic. She felt so tired.

He handed her the drink and sat down in the chair next to hers, their knees touching. Startled at the contact, she shied away suddenly, dropping her glass on the floor, tiny sparkling shards crashing over the tiles, the whisky splashing over one of the rugs. 'Oh!' She stood nervously. 'I'm sorry. I——'

'Calm down, Lora. As you've already told me,' he added sardonically, 'I'm not going to hurt you. I'll go and get a cloth.'

She watched him disappear through the doorway and then saw, on the banister in the hall, his discarded jacket. The keys. Driven more by instinct than any reasoning force, she slipped into the hall and put her hands in his right pocket. Her fingers grasped the cold metal bunch with heart-stopping astonishment. Before she knew what she was doing, she had slipped out of the house and was making for the car. It all seemed so absurdly easy. The first key she tried in the ignition fitted and she turned it with trepidation.

She looked up, her heart hammering at the sudden noise of the engine. It didn't make much, but it seemed to roar in the stillness. Luc was already in the doorway, hurrying down to her. Panic-stricken, she shoved the gearstick forward and stamped on the accelerator. With a tiger snarl the Mercedes jerked backwards, spitting gravel, and crashed into a stone wall. 'What the hell do you think you are trying to do?' Luc had jerked open the door and he was madder than mad.

'I was trying to get away—what did you think I was doing?' muttered Lora, lifting her head from the steering-wheel. Putting a seatbelt on had been the last thing on her mind and now blood was trickling into her eyes.

'You're insane,' he accused, quickly probing the hairline cut.

'You can get arrested for not wearing a seatbelt these days,' said Lora hazily as he half pulled, half carried her out of the car. 'Why don't you call the police and we could go to prison together?'

Luc hooked his arm around her knees and carried her to the house. He looked down at her, his mouth compressed into one grim line. 'I ought to lock you up and throw away the key.'

'Thought you'd already done that,' whispered Lora before she blacked out.

She woke up in her bedroom, a cold compress on her forehead, Luc sitting at the end of the bed gazing at her. 'Have you got a twin brother?' she muttered.

'Why?'

'He's sitting right next to you,' she said. 'Which one is you?'

'I'm the one with the strait-jacket in my hand,' replied Luc grimly. 'And when you wake up properly you are going to wear it to stop me from having a nervous breakdown.'

There was a tap on the door and Maria came in. She beamed sympathetically at Lora and then turned to Luc. 'Phone call for you,' she told him in Italian. 'It is Miss Woods.'

With one quick glance at Lora, Luc got off the bed and made for the door. Answering Maria in the same language, he told her, 'Look after the patient until I get back, will you? She might start telling you strange things—I think her bump on the head has affected her a little.'

Lora stifled the desire to throw a pillow at him. Just you wait, Luc, she told him silently. Think I don't know anything, don't you? Well, I'll show you.

Luc stared at her mutinous expression. 'Is something the matter? Are you in pain?'

'Not at all,' said Lora as innocently as she could. 'Should I be?'

He looked as if he was about to say something and then, shrugging helplessly, left to take his call.

'Maria,' she asked as soon as he was safely out of earshot, 'who is Miss Woods?'

The housekeeper wrinkled up her face in distaste and, wringing out Lora's compress, began sponging the girl's face. 'She is Mr Luc's assistant.'

Something about the inflexion on the last word made Lora gently fend off the woman's hand. 'Assistant?'

'She helps him in business. Accounts and things,' explained Maria vaguely. 'I do not know all that she does, and I would not understand, probably, if I did. She stays in America mostly. She once told me she loved her work far too much ever to take a holiday. And oh, how organised that woman is. But I tell you——' Maria thumped her chest impressively '—she would like to organise much more than that. She would take over Luc's whole life.'

'Can't imagine anybody ordering Luc about,' remarked Lora. 'It must be quite a sight.'

'Julie doesn't order him about,' said Maria. 'She wouldn't dare. But she orders everyone else about. Me included. When she came here last time she told me it was wrong for me to have a rest after lunch. Told me I

should do more exercise, like walk to the shops. I wish
she would take a walk—and not come back. I tell you,
I don't like her.'

Lora snorted with laughter. 'Poor girl.'

'She is not a poor girl,' said Maria. 'She is...' She
stopped, and then her face lit up, and she said very carefully in English, 'A pain in the ass.'

Lora gasped with sudden laughter but the housekeeper gazed back at her seriously. 'I learn all the
American phrases from TV, like "stick it in your ear"
and "eggs easy over". Don't you think they can come
in very useful?'

'Very,' Lora managed, before giving herself up completely to a fit of the giggles. 'Have you tried them on
Luc?'

Maria's eyes narrowed. 'Right at this moment I would
like to try some of those insults on him very much. You
would not believe the tension in this house over that
Mark Todd. God knows, I don't have any love for that
man after what he did to this family, but there was no
need for Mr Luc to snap at me just because I asked who
you were. Can you believe it? After all, you are his girlfriend. He should be happy with a girl like you. But
then——' she shrugged '—it must be true love.'

Lora stared at her, fascinated. 'Why, Maria?'

'Because he is so bad-tempered. All men are like bears
with a sore head when they fall in love.' The housekeeper tapped the side of her nose. 'I know this to be
true. Trust me.'

Lora thought wryly of what Maria would think if she
told her the real truth about her situation. And she was
just about to put her in the picture when she looked up
to see Luc standing in the doorway.

'I must congratulate you on your fluency in Italian,' he said mildly. 'You speak it much better than I.'

Lora looked at him defiantly, her face reddening. 'Thank you. As a matter of fact Maria and I have been having a very interesting conversation about you.'

He turned to the housekeeper and said something curt in French. But Maria stood her ground and said something equally forceful before marching with great dignity from the room.

Luc sat on the bed again and sighed. 'What am I going to do about you, Lora?'

'I don't know,' she said candidly. 'I've been wondering that myself.'

'You will probably be able to go home tomorrow,' he said at last. 'Everything should be sorted out by then.'

'I'm still going to go to the police,' she said. 'Whatever you say.'

He clenched his jaw. 'You can do what you damn well like,' he said.

'B-but,' Lora faltered, 'don't you care?'

'Of course I care,' he grated. 'But I can't stop you. I can't keep you forever. God forbid,' he sighed. 'I'd be a nervous wreck if I tried to act your gaoler for much longer.'

'But you'll go to prison,' said Lora.

'What are you, my defence counsel all of a sudden?' He scowled at her and then got off the bed and began pacing around the room like a caged tiger.

'I took you prisoner because I had to, because there was so much at stake. If Mark Todd thinks he can double-cross me as well as my brother and father, then he can think again. The ink will be dry on some new contracts tomorrow and he can whistle for his country club.'

He rounded on her suddenly. 'And if you think that anything you say or do will alter that, then you can think again too. If I have to go to prison for kidnapping you, well, so be it. When I think of what I have gained it will certainly be worth it.'

Lora glared at him. 'Well, I'm glad you think so. I'm the one who's probably going to lose my job over this. Mark is not exactly the forgiving type. And if you've tricked him as much as you think you have, then nothing on earth will keep him from taking it out on me.'

He stopped in mid-stride by the head of the bed and looked down at her. Her blonde hair framed her elfin face, the cut on her head and smudges under her eyes only serving to accentuate her vulnerability. His fingers reached out slowly and touched her cheek. 'I was going to offer you a job this evening,' he said slowly.

'What as?' said Lora, her pulse jerking at his unexpected touch. 'A get-away driver?'

A ghost of a smile crossed his face. 'I wouldn't last very long as a master criminal if I had you as a get-away driver. I'd be spending most of my time speeding backwards into walls.'

'You certainly know how to insult a girl, don't you?' said Lora. 'For all your professed awkwardness with the English language.'

'I'm trying to help you,' said Luc. 'I have plenty of business interests in England, and I'm sure one of them has a job which could suit your rather special talents.'

Lora struggled to sit upright, her head pounding. 'You can keep your rotten business interests,' she said fiercely. 'If you think you're going to get me to drop any charges against you just by offering me a job, think again. If I'm not bribable with money, I'm certainly not going to be swayed by the offer of slaving in one of your miserable offices.'

Luc sat down on the bed with a thump and grabbed her arms. 'I'm not bribing you, you silly woman,' he roared. 'I am trying to help you.'

'Stop hurting my arms, you beast!' she yelled back. But instead he pulled her towards him until their faces were only inches apart. She could feel his breath hot on her cheek, his eyes boring into hers. Her lips parted and he stopped them with his.

But this was no gentle kiss. This was a male animal claiming his rights. She had to resist or be consumed. But the feel of his lips on her skin was almost more than she could deal with. She felt so overcome with desire that she was in danger of forgetting to breathe.

There was no point in trying to build up any controlled defences where this man was concerned. It was like putting an ice-tray out in the sun and expecting it not to melt.

'What is this?' she gasped at last, running her tongue over her bruised lips. 'A replay of this afternoon? An attempt to pick up where you left off?'

Luc said nothing, only a muscle in his neck giving away the emotions racing under that oh, so steady exterior.

Lora clutched at a pillow for some support. 'You just captured me to further your business plans,' she forced out, willing her heart to stop its thundering roar in her ears. 'But I am not yours to take.'

'Whose are you, then, Lora Seaton?' he asked huskily.

'I am my own woman,' she said, gazing defiantly at him. 'I won't be picked up and put down like a convenient toy, the way you treated me this afternoon.'

Luc pulled her closer to him, and lay down next to her. His eyes were liquid pools, his magnificent body as relaxed as a sleepy panther. 'Would you rather then that I had not, as you say, put you down?'

'You know what I meant,' breathed Lora, her whole being flushing hot at his gaze.

He reached down and lifted her wrist. 'I know only what your body is telling me,' he whispered. 'Or is your pulse racing so because you are afraid of me?'

'I'm not afraid,' blustered Lora.

'Not even in the slightest bit terrified?' he said, mocking her earlier admission on the drive home, his fingers caressing the pulse-point on her wrist with an almost hypnotic rhythm.

'Certainly not,' she swallowed.

'Good,' he replied softly, his hand pulling away the thin blanket covering her. She reached out to pull it back but his hand stayed hers. 'Don't cover yourself up,' he said gently. 'Let me look at you.'

She lay exposed to his gaze, trying not to gasp as his eyes travelled down her pale gold body. 'You are so beautiful, Lora,' he murmured huskily, his hand following where his eyes led.

Instinctively she moved closer to him, her hands moving up under his shirt. 'Your skin feels so lovely,' she said wonderingly. 'Like silk.'

He gave a little snort of laughter. 'Yours is silk too,' he whispered. 'So soft.'

Slowly he undid the buttons of his shirt and then put his arms round her. 'Come here. Close to me,' he said. 'I want to feel your body close to mine.'

Soft skin on hard body. Silk on silk. Lora's thoughts swept together into a whirlpool of desire. All she could see were Luc's eyes, speaking a private silent language only for her. All she could feel was Luc's body drawing out an answering passion from her. A passion that she had so foolishly thought she could hide.

He cupped her breast, but as he bent to kiss a burning trail to its rosy peak one lightning flash of reality broke the magic that held Lora spellbound. He was her captor. She was his prisoner. She could not afford to give in. Could not afford to give him her affection, her body, her love.

Turning away from him with a little cry, she buried her head in the pillow and gasped. 'I can't do this Luc. I can't.'

And, just as if he were a wild animal, his whole body suddenly tensed. The room seemed completely silent.

'Because of Mark Todd?' he rasped.

'M-Mark?' she faltered, and then as the memory of her conversation with Luc that afternoon returned she felt suddenly confused and adrift. What exactly had she said to him?

'Yes, Mark,' he repeated roughly. 'I must admit I was beginning to be flattered that you could forget your lover so easily. Or did you simply sleep with him so that you could get a job?'

'What do you think?' choked Lora, turning to face him.

He felt for the buttons of his shirt. 'I don't know what to think any more,' he said.

'Very well,' said Lora, her spine stiffening with angry defiance at his calm assumption of how she had behaved. 'I slept with him to get a job. And every time I wanted a pay rise I slept with him then too. What do you think of that?'

Her chin up, her eyes suspiciously bright, she glared at Luc, watching him do up his shirt.

Luc nodded. 'All right, Lora. I always did like your sense of humour. But when I was in London I saw you with Mr Todd in a very expensive restaurant. What was he doing, helping you celebrate your latest pay rise?'

Lora's jaw dropped. 'Y-you saw us?' she stammered. 'But——'

'But Mark Todd takes all his junior secretaries to La Cupole for dinner,' said Luc. 'Of course.'

She glared at him. 'Why should I give you an explanation?' she snapped, grabbing for the blanket to cover herself. Damn Luc. Who was he to make her feel so exposed?

'Just who the hell do you think you are?' she demanded out loud.

Luc moved so that his body was covering hers. 'Would you like me to show you?' he said softly.

Lora stared at him, her face set. Silence held them and then was shattered by the doorbell.

'What a popular person you are turning out to be,' she said stonily. 'Maybe it's that nice Miss Woods wanting to check your accounts.'

Luc said nothing, just stared at her, and Lora dropped her gaze and bit her lip. 'I'm sorry,' she muttered. 'That was rather catty of me. I haven't even met the woman.'

For a moment Luc held himself stock-still and then, tipping up her chin, he kissed her gently on her bruised lips. 'That is a promise for later,' he said. 'Whatever your feelings for Mark Todd, there will be a later and we both know it.'

'Not for us,' she said.

He swung himself off the bed and went to the door. As he opened it he turned and looked at her consideringly. 'You are not free yet, Miss Seaton.'

Lora sat up suddenly and grasped a pillow to throw at him, but was stopped by an odd glint in his eyes. 'What's the matter?' she said, suddenly uncertain.

'Nothing,' he replied matter-of-factly as he turned back to rummage in a chest of drawers. 'Which is precisely what you're wearing.'

'Oh!' Lora gasped, clasping the pillow to her body. And then, staring hard at him, she forced out, 'It was you who took my clothes off, wasn't it, when I blacked out?'

He smiled into her accusing eyes. 'Right first time.'

'How could you?' she demanded. 'How could you take advantage like that?'

'Here,' he said, thrusting a T-shirt at her. 'I did it because you were out cold and I needed to make sure you hadn't damaged yourself in any other way, like cracking a few ribs.'

'How very public-spirited of you,' retorted Lora, anger masking the way her heart was thudding at his gaze.

'Very,' he agreed. 'Now, I have no objection at all to seeing you leaping about in the nude with a pillow, but the doctor I've called thinks you have had a nasty crack on the head, and I wouldn't like to let him think he's wasting his time.'

'Oh, go away,' she muttered indistinctly, hiding her reddening face in the cool folds of the T-shirt. She had barely scrambled into it, her head pounding, when Luc brought in the doctor.

CHAPTER SIX

'YES,' the doctor said a few minutes later. 'You were right to call me, Luc. Nothing particularly serious, but she will have to stay quiet for a day or so.'

'A day or so?' yelped Lora. 'I can't stay here that long!'

Luc turned to the doctor. 'I think she means she can't stay still for that long,' he said smoothly.

The man's face cleared. 'Oh. I was beginning to think my English—what little I have of it—was disappearing completely.' He turned to Lora and beamed. 'Nothing much to worry about,' he said. 'But take it easy. You're in good hands here.' He winked theatrically and added, 'It is a long time since Luc brought a girlfriend home. You must be very special. Make sure he looks after you.'

Lora could not meet Luc's eyes as he grasped her hand and said, 'Oh, I will, you can be sure of that.' The nerve of the man. The utter bloody nerve.

She thought of how she had lain in his arms only a few minutes ago, and could feel the colour slowly seep up her neck and face. The more the doctor and Luc gazed at her, the redder and redder she grew, until she felt her cheeks grow almost beetroot with embarrassment.

The doctor was smiling at her, a friendly knowing smile, and she knew exactly what was going through his mind. That she and Luc were lovers. Luc's affectionate tone, her burning embarrassment were only serving to confirm the assumption. It would be impossible to tell this man the truth. He would merely think that her knock on the head was more serious than he had at first diagnosed.

At last Luc ushered the doctor out. When he returned, he leant against the door and stared at her speculatively. 'Tell me something, Lora.'

She wrapped her arms around her knees as if to protect herself from his gaze and then enquired as coolly as she could, 'Name, rank or serial number?'

He gestured impatiently as if clearing away her remark. 'Why didn't you tell the doctor your story?'

She shrugged and then answered bitterly, 'You mean the silly one about how you kidnapped me and are now keeping me prisoner against my will?'

Only the narrowing of his eyes showed that her barb had gone home. 'That's the one,' he nodded calmly. 'Yes.'

She sighed. 'What would be the point? You were quite right, weren't you? If I had turned round to him and said, Thanks so much for looking at my head. Oh, and by the way, this man Luc de la Falaise, whom you seem to have known for years, and who appears to be extremely kind to me, is really keeping me here against my will. How about helping me to escape? you can guess what he would have done.'

Luc smiled a little and answered, 'He would have tut-tutted sympathetically and given me a bottle of pills for your nerves. Of course,' he added, 'considering the way you have been behaving lately, the person who is most in need of nerve pills at the moment is me.'

'They wouldn't do you any good,' replied Lora with a yawn. 'You haven't got any nerves. You don't care about anything except your precious property contracts.'

'Of course not,' agreed Luc, walking to the bed and gazing at her. 'Now lie down and go to sleep.'

For once it seemed surprisingly nice to do just as he told her.

'You know something?' she said sleepily.

'What?'

'This bed is awfully comfortable,' she murmured, sliding down under the sheets with an enormous yawn. 'Maybe I'll escape from you tomorrow,' she added dreamily, sleep claiming her at last.

'I don't really understand what Mark can have done to make you go all out for vengeance like this,' said Lora.

It was the next morning and she was sitting on a sun-lounger by the pool in the shade of a pine tree. Luc had insisted on carrying her out to it and they had eaten breakfast in companionable silence. But the mere mention of Mark's name seemed enough to chase the peaceful look from Luc's face and replace it with the beginnings of a black scowl.

'What Mark did is none of your business,' he began.

'It's become very much my business,' she replied. 'I'm here now because of what has happened between you two, and I want to know why.'

'So you can go straight back to England and tell him?' Luc bit out.

So he still thought Mark was her lover. 'Why not?' she challenged. 'It might enable me to save my job.'

Luc poured himself more coffee and gave her a hard stare.

'Please tell me what he did,' she asked, trying a more neutral appeal. 'I don't want to pry into your private family affairs, but I do think I have the right to know something.'

Luc banged down the cup on the table. 'Mark Todd is nothing more than a bloodsucker,' he said. Then he breathed deeply and stared into space for a few moments before looking back at Lora. 'I suppose you might as well know,' he acknowledged at last.

'The first thing is that I never really got on with my father or my elder brother, Henri.' His lips twisted. 'Maybe I should say they didn't get on with me.

'Don't get me wrong,' he explained. 'We didn't hate each other. They were just two of a kind and no matter what I said I always rubbed them up the wrong way.'

'Two of a kind?' repeated Lora confusedly.

'Like old-time aristocrats,' said Luc tersely. 'I could understand it to a point in my father—he was of a generation that was expected to think that way—but Henri was just the same—charming, indolent, with a complete disdain for all things businesslike. But me, I had ambition for the place. I took a business degree and kept making suggestions, telling them they should do this or that.'

'And what did they think of your ideas?' asked Lora gently.

He shot her a look of disgust. 'Not much. In the end we had the most enormous row and I stormed off determined to show them I wasn't such a fool. I went to New York and worked on Wall Street——'

'Where all the bars were made of gold,' remembered Lora.

'Correct,' said Luc with a grim smile. 'I had the skill, granted. But I always seemed to have a huge amount of luck too. Unlike my family.'

'Did you go home to them at all?' she asked.

Luc shook his head. 'Too proud. I had made a lot of money, but it never seemed enough. I wanted to really rub their faces in it. When I did contact them, they told me they were doing perfectly well and to get back to my money-grubbing. Stupidly, I did just that. And then just after I awarded myself a few months off to explore South America they were killed in a car crash.'

He looked at Lora, his face bleak. 'I mean, I didn't find out about it until long afterwards when I returned. And then what a discovery I made! The whole place was mortgaged up to the hilt to a Swiss bank and Mark Todd had made an offer which those jackass executives accepted! They said it was the best deal all round. Apparently Henri had signed papers he shouldn't have and the only thing I was going to get was what was left after the bank had had its share. To argue for anything else would have taken years, with the whole place going to ruin.

'I got them to agree finally that if Mark didn't sign on the dotted line at the time allotted, which he had to do anyway under French law, then I would get first refusal.'

Lora sighed. 'And that's where I came in, wasn't it?'

Luc nodded. 'Yes, unfortunately for you.'

She wrinkled her forehead. 'I still don't understand why you hate Mark so much. Surely it is not unreasonable to expect that a businessman would want to buy the place?'

'Mark Todd is not just any businessman,' ground out Luc. 'He was the man who lent Henri vast amounts of money at a huge rate of interest in the first place. And when Henri couldn't pay, Mark expected to be given the property in lieu. Fortunately, for the first and last time in his life, my brother had a tiny inkling of common sense and signed the place over to the bank instead.'

'And then they died,' said Lora quietly. She sighed and then smiled sympathetically at him. 'You haven't really had a very fortunate time, have you?'

Luc glared at her. 'Are you trying to be funny?' he demanded.

'No,' she gasped. 'Certainly not.'

A muscle throbbed in his cheek and he stood up abruptly. 'I have business to attend to. You can stay here for the rest of the morning.'

'Thanks,' gritted Lora.

'It was an order, not an invitation,' snarled Luc. 'Just do me one favour.'

'What?'

'Try not to fall in the swimming-pool today, will you?'

Lora glared at him but he had already turned his back and was making for the house.

She lay back in the sun-lounger with a sigh. Luc's story had given her a lot to think about and with her head still aching she wasn't sure where to begin. It was so hot. Maybe she could think better with her eyes closed.

In a few minutes she was fast asleep.

'And who exactly are you?' The brisk American accent reached down into Lora's dreams and she woke with a start.

'What?' she said sleepily, opening her eyes and realising that a stranger was staring at her impatiently.

'I said,' came the efficient, waspish voice again, 'who are you? Because if you're that maid Maria was thinking about employing you are fired, as of this moment. And I don't care what Luc says.'

Lora sat up quickly and gazed at the woman standing in front of her. She was an attractive brunette somewhere in her late twenties and she was wearing a severely cut blue suit, not unlike the one Lora herself had worn the day before, topped off with an imperious expression.

'Hello,' said Lora with a sleepy smile.

'Don't "hello" me,' said the woman impatiently. 'I don't care for laziness and you might as well know it.'

Lora lay back luxuriously in her lounger and positively beamed at the stranger. 'Something tells me you must be Julie Woods, right?'

'Never mind who I am,' the woman replied. 'Who are you, and what are you doing lying around when there are rooms to be cleaned?'

'I thought you'd just fired me,' said Lora innocently, smiling up into Julie's glacier gaze. The other woman opened her mouth to say something else when she was forestalled by a deep, familiar voice.

'Julie,' said Luc, walking up to them in his swimming-trunks, beads of water glittering on his face and chest. 'I don't think you've met my girlfriend Lora, have you?'

'What?' gasped Julie. Lora's jaw dropped, but after a day or so in Luc's company she had somehow got beyond gasping.

'Hello, darling, have a nice sleep?' Luc bent to kiss her on the cheek, his face cool against her hot skin after his swim.

'I'm going to kill you,' muttered Lora.

'In gaol or out?' replied Luc, just as softly.

'Luc,' said Julie briskly, 'I came today because I figured you could use a hand with this New York report. The projections are completely haywire.'

'That was good of you,' said Luc in a deceptively mild tone.

'But I have a problem,' she added, pointing at Lora's window. 'The room I usually use has got someone else's stuff all over it.'

'Well, I could easily move out,' said Lora, with a wicked smile at Luc. 'In fact, I should have left several days ago.'

Their eyes locked, her expression signalling, How are you going to get out of this one, then?

Luc smiled at her lazily. His eyes never left her face as he replied to Julie, 'No problem at all. Lora can come back into my room tonight.'

'What?' exclaimed Lora, feeling as though she had just stepped into a lift shaft.

'I knew you'd like the good news,' he told her silkily. And then, turning to Julie, he explained, 'Lora's not been very well recently. She needed some uninterrupted nights' sleep so I gave her your room. Knew you wouldn't mind.'

'Not at all,' said Julie briskly, and then, gazing alertly at both of them, asked, 'So you two are an item, then?'

'You could say that,' agreed Luc.

'You can't have known each other for long,' objected Julie.

'Ages,' said Lora unthinkingly. Then, catching a glint in Luc's eye, she realised what she had said. She had known him for only a couple of days yet it seemed as though she had known him all her life. 'Actually,' she amended, 'it's less time than I thought, but then they do say time goes fast when you're enjoying yourself.'

Julie gave her a strange look and then turned to Luc. 'You gonna name the day?' she said almost skittishly.

'It has to be real serious for you, Luc, if you've brought her to your home here.'

'The day?' repeated Lora, a horrible suspicion forming in her mind.

Luc grasped her hand and smiled right down into her eyes. 'You know, darling, our wedding-day. When's suitable for you?'

Lora glared at him, and as he bent to kiss her cheek again she hissed in his ear, 'You are completely off your rocker.'

'Funny,' he mused. 'That's exactly what the doctor said about you.'

It was late afternoon and Lora had spent most of it relaxing on the lounger by the pool, the heat and the after-effects of her crack on the head making her feel sleepy and rather woolly-minded.

The way Luc had got the better of her in front of Julie nagged at her like a sore tooth, but, no matter how her brain struggled to come up with a solution to her deepening problems, no ready answer appeared.

She just didn't physically feel up to trying to escape again, and, more to the point, she couldn't see how. But one thing was absolutely certain: she was not going to be sharing Luc's bed tonight.

After she had met Julie, Luc and his assistant had gone into the house to tackle business. He had spent several hours closeted with her going over the New York report, whatever that was, but now, as the shadows lengthened over the poolside, he emerged from the house with two cool drinks.

'Here,' he said, handing one to Lora and sitting by her side.

Lora sipped it gratefully and then looked at him. 'Did you mean what you said about me being in your room tonight?' she asked, trying hard to sound matter-of-fact.

He looked steadily out over the fields towards the château. 'Of course,' he shrugged, turning back to gaze at her. 'Why not?'

'Why not?' she gasped. 'Look here, Mr de la Falaise, you can just get one thing straight right now,' she told him furiously. 'I am not going to sleep with you and that's final! Just what sort of a person do you take me for?'

Luc gazed at her. 'A kidnap victim,' he said mildly. 'And, more to the point, my kidnap victim. What else?'

'You could have put me in another room,' she snapped. 'This house is enormous.'

'I could not,' he replied. 'The room you have spent the last two nights in is the only one I feel safe putting you in. The others all offer possibilities of escape. I only came back to this house a few weeks ago and there are renovations that need doing all over. Especially in the bedrooms.'

'But you don't lock me in!' retorted Lora. 'So what difference does it make?'

'I locked you in last night,' he said calmly. 'I thought you might try sleepwalking your way to freedom.'

Her jaw dropped. 'You did what?'

'Standard procedure, I should think, in such cases,' he informed her sardonically. 'Especially after the escape attempts you have made.'

'I'll give you standard procedure...' she threatened.

'Is that a promise for tonight?' he drawled. 'I can hardly wait.'

She glared at his lazily good-natured expression and bit her lip. There was absolutely no way of getting the better of this man. 'I'm not going to sleep in your room tonight,' she repeated at last. 'And that's final.'

'Good,' he smiled. 'Sleep was the last thing on my mind.'

'It's the first thing on mine,' snapped Lora.

'Really?' he enquired. 'You surprise me. I would have thought you had had enough sleep lately to keep you going for the next week or so. I know the doctor said you should rest, but for a moment or two today I thought you had gone into hibernation.' He smiled at her. 'Perhaps you were a dormouse in a former life.'

'I feel more like a bear with a sore head,' said Lora grimly. 'So don't push your luck.'

Luc's eyes glinted. 'On the contrary, *chérie*, it is your luck that you are pushing. You are lucky I am such a patient man.'

Lora glared at him and bit her lip. When would she learn to be more conciliatory towards this man? 'I can't help feeling sleepy,' she said at last. 'I expect it's an after-effect of the accident, and I didn't get a great deal of sleep before I came on this trip.'

Luc gazed at her in mock-sympathy. 'Your wonderful Mr Todd has obviously been keeping you up.'

Lora flushed at the implication of his remark. 'That's unfair,' she retorted.

'On the contrary,' he said. 'I think it was a very fair remark in the circumstances.'

'You know nothing at all about my circumstances,' Lora spat. 'And don't you dare judge me. You are not exactly squeaky clean yourself. You're...' She paused for breath. 'You're nothing more than a kidnapper. And you can't get much lower than that.'

'Oh, but you can, Lora,' replied Luc. 'I advise you to take a long look at Mark Todd when you get back. You would have to dig a very deep pit indeed to get much lower than him.'

She glared at him but he merely shrugged. 'It is true, Lora. I am surprised you have not found that out already.'

Lora opened her mouth to tell him the exact truth and then closed it again. She simply could not afford to tell Luc more than she had to. It would make her position even more vulnerable and he was not a man to ignore an advantage, no matter how trivial.

The silence stretched between them, both busy with their own thoughts. In the end it was Luc who spoke first, and with a perfectly ordinary question. 'What do you want for dinner tonight?' he asked, tacitly agreeing that they should change the subject.

'Bread and water,' retorted Lora. 'Isn't that standard fare for prisoners?'

'Not unless they prefer stuffed pigs' feet,' replied Luc with some amusement.

'If I break my glass,' Lora said tartly, 'maybe I can put the bits in your food. That is, if Julie doesn't have to taste everything you eat first.'

His hand closed over hers. 'I do believe you are jealous of Julie.'

'I am not jealous,' she snapped, a trifle too quickly. 'Why should I be?'

He shrugged. 'No reason at all, except that we work quite closely together. A lot of people thought we'd get married.'

A small knot tightened in Lora's stomach. She lifted her eyes to his, but his expression was completely unreadable. 'Why didn't you?' she asked in spite of herself.

'Long story,' he said blandly, his sharp eyes taking in every nuance of her expression.

Her jaw clenched. 'Well, why don't you sleep with her tonight, then?' she grated. 'And then I can have her room and all of us will be happy.'

His eyes glimmered with amusement. 'Oh, but I couldn't do that, Lora. After all, I'd be worrying all the time about where you were. Whether you had fallen off a drainpipe, maybe, or got yourself knotted up in some sheets, or even if perhaps you had succeeded in completely mangling the gearbox on the Mercedes.'

He stretched his long legs out more comfortably and then turned to her again. 'Tell me, what form is your next escape attempt going to take?'

'Hot-air balloon,' she snapped. 'What else?'

He looked at her interestedly. 'Are you going to power it yourself?'

She swung her legs off the lounger at that and stormed off angrily, his laughter ringing in her ears as she headed for the house.

It didn't help that when she got to what had been her room there was no sign of any of her meagre possessions.

'Oh, Luc had them taken to his room,' explained Julie, looking up from a long sheet of figures and hurriedly laying another sheet of paper over them.

'Well, where is that?' demanded Lora. What was the matter with this woman? Anyone would think from her behaviour that she thought she was being spied on.

Julie took off her glasses and rubbed a small red mark on the bridge of her nose. 'You mean you don't know?'

she said incredulously. 'My, but you two really must be serious.'

'It's the crack on my head,' snapped Lora. 'This house is so damned big and I just can't seem to remember the most simple things.'

Julie got up at that and stepped towards her. 'I'll show you, if you like,' she offered. 'I'm going out anyway and I can point you in the right direction.'

Lora looked at her thoughtfully. 'You came in your own car, then?' she said casually.

'Oh, yes,' replied Julie. 'I couldn't do my job very efficiently without one.'

'You couldn't give me a lift into town?' suggested Lora as nonchalantly as she could, her heart beating a nervous tattoo. Perhaps this was her chance to be free at last. To escape from Luc and all the complicated feelings he aroused in her.

Julie smiled at her and shook her head. 'Luc said you might ask me that.'

'He did?' said Lora, her heart dropping. 'What did he say exactly?'

'He said you were far too active for your own good at the moment. Always trying to rush around doing things.' Julie stepped a pace closer. 'You really must take it easy, you know. Luc said the doctor told him you were to have complete quiet. He said going anywhere was absolutely out of the question—for the time being, of course.'

'He said that, did he?' asked Lora with dangerous calm.

'Yes,' Julie confirmed innocently. 'He said you were lucky only to have been involved in a relatively minor crash. Said some sort of maniac had been driving.' She

'Of course not,' he said lightly. 'And it was naturally all my fault for letting you jump to a conclusion about what was going to happen tonight, Lora.' He shrugged. 'And I thought it was all wishful thinking on your part.'

The gleam of humour in his eyes was just too much. 'Wishful thinking!' she quavered defiantly. 'Don't be so silly.'

His fingers trailed down her cheek and he smiled wryly at her. 'I guess I was interested in your reaction so I let you think what you liked for longer than I should have.'

'It seems my behaviour has just made you jump to some ridiculous conclusions,' she breathed, wishing desperately that she could sound more convincing.

'Oh, yes,' he replied. 'It made me jump to some very silly conclusions indeed, like if it weren't for the fact you need some sleep I probably would be sharing this bed with you tonight.'

She opened her mouth, but before she could say anything he reached down and kissed her swiftly on the lips. 'Goodnight, Lora. Sleep well.'

'I won't,' she replied mutinously.

'Oh, I should if I were you,' he informed her. 'After all, you might dream about me. And I'm much safer in dreams than in real life.'

She looked wildly about for something to throw at him but the door had closed behind him with a soft click and she could hear him laughing all the way down the landing.

It was quite dark when she woke up. She looked at her watch. Midnight. Her head pounding, she got up and made for the door. She simply had to have a glass of water.

There was a light on downstairs and she made for it. It was coming from the sitting-room, and when she put her head round the door she could see Luc in an armchair gazing at the empty hearth. There were business papers piled high on the table beside him and his face was grim. She made as if to tiptoe away, thinking that he hadn't seen her, but he raised his eyes to hers and lifted a hand. 'Come in, Lora.'

She walked up to him. 'Before you ask,' she said as confidently as she could, 'I was just looking for a glass of water, not a new escape route.'

'Glad to hear it,' he said absently.

'Luc?' questioned Lora. 'Is something the matter?'

He sighed. 'Business. I don't think, in all my life, I've seen such a tangled mess as this.' He rubbed his fingers across his forehead and yawned.

'Your brother seems to have caused you a lot of trouble,' remarked Lora.

'My brother?' said Luc. He looked at Lora as if he hadn't heard her properly and then added softly. 'Oh, Henri. Yes, I see what you mean.'

Lora gave him a strange look. He must be even tireder than he had at first seemed. 'Maybe you should go on a holiday when all this is over,' she suggested.

Luc's lips curved into a smile. 'If you have anything to do with it, I expect I shall be having a very long holiday, at Her Majesty's pleasure.'

Lora flushed. 'Maybe,' she said, and then added quickly, 'How about a hot drink?'

'Wonderful.' He smiled at her as she made for the kitchen. 'Only...'

She turned. 'Yes?'

'Not tea. It's one of the few English habits that I really loathe.'

She nodded, and then, determined not to give him the upper hand, said as tartly as she could, 'You get a lot of tea in prison, Luc. And I hope for your sake that you like porridge.'

Once in the kitchen, Lora poured a jug of milk into a saucepan and then, without turning around, knew that Luc had followed her.

'You look as if you have enough tins of hot chocolate there to feed an army,' he said.

'No. Just you and me,' she replied. 'One of them was nearly empty. So I opened another. What's the matter?' she added as an afterthought. ''Fraid I might be going to steal some of it to use as escape rations?'

He moved swiftly to her and put his hands on her shoulders. His nearness was almost more than she could bear. The warmth from his fingers radiated through her dress and spread over her skin. She wanted so desperately to turn around and touch him but instead gritted her teeth and bent her head. Her throat tightened and her eyes blurred as she willed herself not to break down as she had after dinner. Weeping was just not her style. But her tears began to fall in the milk as she stirred it more and more haphazardly.

'Stop this, Lora,' he said harshly. 'You know as well as I do how we're beginning to feel about each other.'

'Do I?' she replied woodenly.

He turned her to face him, her wooden spoon clattering on to the floor. 'Yes, you do,' he said before pulling her into his arms and kissing her. She struggled at first to push him away but his body was too strong and his attraction too powerful. In the end it was he who stopped, holding her still with his arms and his black stare. 'Tell me you don't want this, Lora,' he said huskily. 'Tell me that you don't want me.'

'You know I can't,' she replied in a low voice. 'But as you've already told me, you have all the aces. You're my kidnapper, Luc. I'm your captive and it doesn't matter what you say—I just can't forget that. To give in to you now would be like...' She shrugged helplessly.

'Like giving in?' said Luc softly.

She nodded. 'Yes. And I won't give in. Ever. You can take my body but I won't let you have my soul. Not like this. I just can't.'

'If I gave you your freedom now, would you go?' he asked softly.

She rubbed a hand wearily across her forehead. Behind them the milk boiled over with a hiss, and Luc reached behind her to switch off the gas, his eyes never leaving Lora's face.

'Well?' he prompted.

'I don't know,' she said quietly. 'How can I tell until I have the choice?'

He sighed and then, reaching into his pocket, he pulled out her passport, ticket and his wallet. 'Here,' he said, handing her the documents and then extracting a thick wad of notes from his wallet. 'Take them.'

Lora looked numbly at him and then he grasped her hand and closed her fingers over the little bundle. 'You're free, Lora. Free to go wherever you like. What is your choice? Do you want to go?'

It was as if she had fallen through a trap-door. Was she really free? Silently she nodded without looking up into his face. 'Yes,' she replied at last. 'I think that would be the best thing. I'll go whenever's convenient.'

It was as if they were discussing a business appointment. Lora longed for him to contradict her, to tell her she must stay. But he merely ran the back of one of his fingers down her tear-stained cheek and murmured huskily, 'I was wrong to keep you captive. It was like putting a wild bird in a cage; but at the time I thought it was worth it.'

'And was it?' asked Lora.

'I suppose I did achieve some of my aims. I taught that cheat Mark Todd a lesson and...' He shrugged.

'Made a pile of money?' finished Lora bitterly.

He looked at her with an odd glint in his eye. 'I was going to say and I met you.'

'Oh,' said Lora. It was the last thing she would have expected him to come out with. He seemed so utterly self-sufficient that she had never thought he would have any particular feelings about anyone, least of all herself.

'If anything,' he continued, 'I lost money on the deal. But, as you told me at the *auberge*, there are some things that are more important than cold cash.'

She looked down at her hand as if she had never seen it before. Was she really free again? 'Why are you giving me all this money?' she asked. 'I certainly didn't come with that much.'

'It is yours now,' he told her. 'It cannot make up for your being held here against your will, but it might help you out, if Mark ditches you.'

She looked at him in some confusion at that. The word 'ditch' was an odd one to use for being sacked, and then light dawned. He still thought Mark was her lover. 'I——' she began.

'No,' he said, tipping up her chin with a gentle forefinger. 'Don't give me all that rubbish about how you cannot accept my money. If it is the only thing of mine that you can take, then take it.'

'But Luc, I have to explain,' she began. 'There are some things you need to know.'

He sighed and turned away. 'I don't want explanations of your relationship with him. What would be the point of them now? If he can keep you while you are free, I can't force you to be mine while you are my captive.'

Lora opened her mouth, but before she could say anything he cut in, 'You are free to go, Miss Seaton. With my compliments.'

He walked to the door and then turned around. 'You can leave now, if you wish. I think that would probably be the best thing. There is a flight in two hours' time. I could get you on that, if you like.'

Lora nodded numbly. 'I suppose so,' she said. It was as if now she had accepted her freedom he couldn't wait to send her away. 'I can't really take all this in.' And as she stared at him once more her heart took a nose-dive. Was she really going away from him?

'Will you drive me there?' she asked in a low voice.

'No.' He shook his head. 'It would only serve to prolong something that should finish with a clean break. Besides,' he added with a grim smile, 'the back lights of the Mercedes, which you smashed in your last escape attempt, will not be fixed by the garage people until tomorrow.' He paused and then told her, 'I'll call a taxi for you.'

'It's a bit late, isn't it?' ventured Lora.

Luc raised an eyebrow and smiled ironically. 'Do you want to leave or don't you?'

'Yes, of course I do; it's just a bit sudden, that's all,' said Lora helplessly. 'I didn't expect it all to turn out like this.'

His eyes glinted. 'You mean it's not being done in accordance with your kidnappers' guidebook?'

'Something like that,' Lora replied, walking towards a kitchen chair and sitting down with a bump.

'Well, you can write a whole new chapter for it now,' said Luc. 'I'll go and ring Jean Poitu, our village odd-job man, and see if he is in a fit state to dig out that metal carcass he calls a taxi and bring it round.'

She sat on the chair and watched him walk out of the door and out of her life. Slowly she got up and, taking a cloth, began to wipe up the lava flow of milk on top of the stove. She could hear Luc speaking rapidly on the telephone and then, quite clearly in the quiet house, she heard the click of the receiver and then silence.

But he did not return to the kitchen. If she was honest she had not really expected him to. Numbly she walked to the kitchen sink, wrung out the cloth and dried her hands on the rough roller towel.

The whole situation was unreal. One moment she was a captive and the next she was free, whatever that meant. But would she ever be free of Luc and the memory of the way he had looked at her, the way he had touched her?

Slowly she walked through to the front hall, to see Luc putting her overnight bag down by the door. 'Packing is not my strong point,' he said to her. 'I just put in everything of yours that I could see.' He took a step towards her. 'I rescued your shoes and that appalling suit of yours, you know. I even got Maria to press it.'

'That was good of you,' said Lora mechanically.

'Very good, considering what it really needs is putting on a bonfire,' nodded Luc.

'Julie wears one just like it,' Lora told him, her eyes never leaving his.

'Does she?' he said. 'I've never noticed.'

The air between them was thick with unsaid things that now, it seemed, never could be said. Except with their eyes.

'I'm glad you got your land back,' she told him. Why was it that only trivialities were springing to her lips when all she wanted to do was tell him how she really felt?

'Luc...' she began, and then faltered. His face looked so grim. Perhaps his approaches to her really had meant nothing to him. No. The way he had treated her had meant something. She would stake her life on it.

'*Au revoir*, Lora,' he said. 'Your taxi is here.'

'Goodbye, Luc,' she breathed, and then, as he opened the door, she lifted her head up and walked out into the night towards the waiting taxi.

It was only at the gateway that she at last twisted round in her seat to watch Luc's tall figure, his arm upraised in farewell, as they drove away. And she stayed looking back long after she could no longer see him.

'Goodbyes are always sad,' said Jean sympathetically. He was a little wrinkled old man who seemed not at all upset at being dragged out of his bed to drive her to the airport.

'*Au revoir* is certainly sad,' said Lora.

'*Au revoir*? *Non*. That is not really sad. It means till we meet again.'

Lora's heart twisted, and she suddenly knew exactly what she had to do if she was not going to live the rest of her life in regret. 'Jean,' she asked, 'do you think we could turn around and go back?'

'*Mais oui*,' shrugged the old man. 'Why not?' And without pausing for thought he manoeuvred the big old car through a startling U-turn with a great crashing of gears. 'Women,' he muttered. 'They are always forgetting something.'

Luc was just opening the door as Lora ran up the steps and went full tilt into him. 'Oh!' she cried, but there was no room for any more words because his lips were on hers, his arms pulling her close.

'Oh, Luc,' she cried at last, 'the taxi driver is still waiting. He thinks I've forgotten something.'

'And have you?' Luc murmured in her hair.

'Only my heart,' said Lora, finally falling into the full black depths of his gaze. 'And probably my head as well.'

'I think Jean has got the message,' Luc told her at last. 'He is pulling away.'

'Gone?' replied Lora wildly, half turning round. 'But he had my suitcase in the back!'

'Good,' said Luc, pulling her back into his arms. 'That scratchy suit will be much nicer on him than on you.'

He led her through the door and closed it behind them. 'Come,' he said simply. 'Let's go to bed.'

'Luc,' she said, staring up at him, 'I'm still free, aren't I?' She was unable to stop the quick rush of nerves at what she had done.

He looked at her and smiled softly. 'As free as air, Lora.'

'Good,' she said, trying hard to disguise the tremble in her voice. 'I had to come back, I——'

'Hush,' he said. 'No more explanations.' And, taking her hand, he led her up the stairs.

Her heart was beating so loudly she was sure he could hear it. Her sexual experiences so far had been nothing to write home about. And now here she was practically throwing herself at Luc. Was she even now making a fool of herself?

Her fingers gripped his more tightly. Had she really done the right thing? She felt the warm comfort flow from his hand and knew without a shadow of a doubt that she had. Everything would be all right. She knew it. And then, almost as if it were a slow-motion film, something happened which turned her to ice where she stood at the top of the landing.

For there, coming out of Luc's room, was Julie. And she was wearing nothing much more than a simple towelling bathrobe.

She stared at Lora as if she were a ghost. 'I thought you'd gone,' she managed at last.

Luc drew Lora more closely towards him and tucked her arm through his. 'Only for a short while,' he said mildly, smiling down at Lora's frozen face.

She tried to pull away but Luc held her fast. 'Goodnight, Julie,' he said firmly.

Julie nodded, the confusion all too evident on her face. 'Well, thanks for the shower, Luc,' she said awkwardly. 'Goodnight.'

Lora felt herself turn from ice to fire. She didn't know whether she wanted to leap at Julie with all the snapping, heat-surging pain that was pounding through her blood, or run screaming down the stairs and out of the house and away forever.

But before she could do anything Luc had marched her into his room and closed the door behind them. Once inside she wrenched her arm free and stalked away from him.

'I think I have a right to know what that woman was doing in your room,' she said, turning to face him.

Luc folded his arms and leant against the door. 'You really care, don't you?' he remarked.

'Of course I——' began Lora, her eyes blazing. And then she stopped. Why should she sacrifice any more pride for this man? 'I don't give a damn what you've been up to,' she said at last, sitting limply on the bed.

'That is not true,' said Luc, unfolding his arms and coming to sit beside her.

'Don't you dare touch me,' yelled Lora, her nerves as taut as piano wire.

'Lora,' he said gently. 'What Julie said was true. She came in to use the shower. Although I suspect she may also have wanted to look at some business papers of mine.'

'Business papers!' retorted Lora bitterly. 'Oh, yes, very believable.'

Luc shrugged. 'It is the truth.' He looked at her angry face and then added mischievously, 'You have hardly been gone any time at all. And Julie did not return to the house until a few minutes after you left. I would have to be a very fast worker indeed if all your suspicions are true.'

'Maybe you'd just got started,' snarled Lora. 'I'm sorry if I interrupted anything.'

'The only thing you interrupted was Julie's shower,' replied Luc.

Lora gazed at him dully. 'You can't begin to understand how much I'd like to believe you, but you know as well as I that there is no shower in this room.'

CHAPTER EIGHT

LORA looked around at the bare walls of the simple room, her heart sagging. 'How could Julie possibly have a shower in this room, Luc?' she sighed wearily. 'Where do you keep it? Under the bed? Or maybe you expect me to believe that she just up-ended that bowl—the one you use for shaving—over her head?'

Luc put his hand under her chin and turned her face to his. 'You should only mock people when you are absolutely sure of your own ground, Lora. Especially when your mockery is tantamount to calling me a liar. Is that what you think I am?'

She stared unwillingly into his eyes and swallowed as his black gaze bored into her. Why had she ever decided to come back to Luc? She would have been better off stepping into a cage with a man-eating tiger.

'Yes, of course I'm calling you a liar,' she said at last. 'I don't know why you bother to deny it. You must admit the evidence against you is pretty damning.'

'I am not going to admit anything,' said Luc calmly. 'All you have done is see Julie in a bathrobe and then jump to a conclusion which is so far from the truth that it would be laughable if I did not feel so seriously about you.'

'Don't try and soft-talk me, Luc,' Lora said wearily. 'I've heard it all before.'

'No doubt from when you had that half-baked affair with your college lecturer,' Luc replied drily.

Lora reddened angrily. 'If you must know, yes,' she flashed. 'And I'm fed up with falling for men who think I'll fall for their lies too.'

A muscle began to pulse in Luc's cheek. 'You must have fallen so much that you've injured your mental processes,' he grated. 'Is that why Mark Todd is now your lover?'

Lora looked at him and said nothing. She felt like choking on the words that came to her lips. Every single thing that pointed to Luc and Julie's having an affair was like a knife going into her heart, but she had to go on, had to lay it all out for him to see. She wanted so much to say nothing, to believe him unconditionally, but the doubts in her soul kept urging her on.

'You said you were involved once,' Lora forced out. 'Why shouldn't you still be attracted to each other? And apart from anything else,' she added bitterly, 'Julie's hair was bone-dry.'

Luc gazed up at the ceiling and sighed deeply before turning back to her. 'I said that people expected us to have something going between us, not that there was. We just worked together. And as for her hair, there are such things as shower caps, you know.'

They stared at each other in silence, and Luc was the first to break it. 'I am not going to quarrel with you over something as silly as this,' he said softly.

Her heart felt as though it was breaking up into huge leaden lumps. 'No,' she choked. 'Let's not have anything as messy as a quarrel. You said I was free—well, I've changed my mind about not going tonight. Just give me the number of that taxi and I'll be out of your and Julie's hair just as soon as I can.'

He grabbed her arms and looked at her exasperatedly. 'You are not going anywhere tonight,' he said. 'Now look over there. You see that door, the one next to the chimney-breast?'

'The cupboard door?' she said dully. Why did he have to prolong the agony, when he only had to admit the obvious truth of what she had said?

'Yes, the cupboard door,' he said slowly and deliberately. 'Now go over there and open it before we both start saying things we'll regret.'

She stared at him, stiff in his arms. 'Why should I?' she demanded, and then, lifting her chin, added, 'No, I won't do it. I won't play this game of yours, Luc. It's all over and it was silly to imagine there was anything between us in the first place. Let's just admit it and leave it at that.'

'And I thought you were such a fighter,' said Luc softly.

'Not for such a lost cause,' replied Lora miserably.

In answer Luc dropped his hands and, getting up, strode to the door.

'What are you doing?' quavered Lora, turning to follow him with her eyes. She was kneeling on the bed now, half poised to make a run for it, if it came to that.

'I'm going to show you some sense,' he retorted, his hand on the door, which was not more than five feet high and very narrow. 'Allow me to demonstrate, *mademoiselle*,' he said coldly, and, bowing low, he yanked open the door.

Without even realising it Lora stood up on the bed, her mouth dropping open in shock. 'It's a shower-room,' she gasped.

'The very same,' agreed Luc drily.

'I thought it was a cupboard,' she whispered.

'So I gathered,' replied Luc. 'Do you always let appearances deceive you?'

'But I saw you shaving in that old-fashioned basin this afternoon,' she objected.

'True,' said Luc. 'The shower-room means just that. There is no basin.'

Their eyes met and he strode to the side of the bed and put his arms out. 'Come here, you exasperating woman.'

He lifted her off the bed, her arms round his neck, her legs around his waist, and carried her to the door. 'I'm sorry, Luc,' she mumbled, not daring to look at his face.

'I should think so,' he murmured, kissing the tip of her nose. 'I admit that Julie coming out of my room like that was a very suspicious sight. But perhaps you will agree now that there was a very innocent explanation. I would not have led you up the stairs if I had had anything to hide.'

'Are there no other bathrooms in this house?' said Lora, staring at the odd arrangement.

'None that works, unfortunately.' Luc smiled at her. 'In most things I will back the French way, but when it comes to plumbing I have spent enough time in New York to realise that perhaps the rest of the world could show us a thing or two in this department.

'You will have to make your own way through, *chérie*,' he added gently, lowering her to the floor. 'This doorway was not meant for two to get through at once.'

Lora stood on the threshold, her arm still around his neck. 'You practically have to go in sideways, don't you?' she breathed. 'But it looks really roomy inside.'

'It was once part of the attic,' explained Luc, following her into the spacious room. 'I think it was one of our tenants who decided to knock the original cupboard out to the attic beyond. The plumbing in this house is completely crazy,' he added. 'But you should see the arrangements at the château. A nightmare. At least here the shower works. It is the only one that does.'

'So you do own the château,' breathed Lora.

'Tomorrow I will,' agreed Luc. 'Tomorrow at last I sign the contract. It is a very odd feeling to buy the home where you grew up and where all your ancestors lived and died.'

'But you said yesterday that it belonged to strangers,' objected Lora.

'Perhaps I should have said Swiss bankers,' said Luc. 'In any case I did not like to say too much. I have it within my grasp but I do not hold it yet.'

He turned her to face him. 'That is enough talking about property deals, I think,' he said softly. 'I thought you wanted to see my shower?'

It was positioned in a tiled alcove. 'No curtains,' said Lora, her heart beating wildly at Luc's closeness.

'No need,' he said softly. 'What do we have to hide?'

'Nothing,' she whispered. 'Not any more.'

'Turn around, Lora, I want to see you,' he ordered huskily. His arms were already encircling her, and as she turned her face to his Luc's hand eased down her zip and pushed the straps of her dress over her shoulders. It fell to the floor and she stood tall, gazing at his face as his eyes travelled down her body. Slowly she unfastened her bra and let that fall too. Lifting her face for a kiss, she stroked her hands up his shoulders and to the nape of his neck. Her body shuddered with desire as his hands moved down the satin length of her spine and his lips caressed her mouth, her throat, her breasts.

Reaching behind her, he switched on the shower and Lora gasped as the full strength of the water hit them. His body crowded hers into the wall as his lips plundered hers, warm water streaming down their faces.

His eyes never leaving hers, he stepped back a little and stripped away her briefs before taking off his own clothes. 'Come, *chérie*,' he then said huskily, turning off the taps. 'I think we can find somewhere more comfortable than cold tiles to make love.'

Taking her by the hand, he led her unresisting from the room, back to his bed. He pulled back the quilt and lay down on the crisp linen sheet. 'Lie next to me, Lora,' he said, pulling her to him, the linen softening under the weight of their damp bodies. 'And we will finish what we both have started.'

Lora awoke in the early morning coolness to see Luc's head on the pillow next to hers, and she smiled sleepily as she remembered how he had made love to her. Had it been only a few hours ago? Wonderingly she put out her fingers and touched the nape of his neck. Had it really happened? Was she really here? As if in answer to the questions crowding her brain, his hand grasped her fingers and he turned to her, pulling her body on top of his. 'No, Luc,' she gasped as he cupped her breast. 'We can't.'

'Can't? he smiled, caressing its hardening pink tip. 'Why not?'

'I . . .' Lora stopped.

Laughing, he tipped her on to her back and leant over her. 'You don't look as if you can think of any reason why we should not make love again,' he said.

'You're right,' sighed Lora. 'I can't. But——'

'No buts,' he said huskily, gathering her into his arms once more.

Later, much later, as they dressed, Lora glanced out of the window. 'That's strange,' she commented. 'Julie's sitting by the pool. I thought she was always rushing about doing this and that.'

Luc gave her an odd look. 'Perhaps she finds that she has to think her next move through very carefully. It is good she is there. I want to talk to her.'

Lora, only half listening, pulled on one of his T-shirts. 'This will do as a dress,' she said. 'But it can't possibly have been this big originally.'

'I think it stretched when it was washed,' said Luc. 'Laundry is really not one of Maria's strong points.'

Lora took a tie from his wardrobe and decided to use it as a belt. 'What do you think?' she asked, holding it up. Luc gazed at her, his eyes sooty black.

'You know what I think,' he said huskily. 'Come here.'

Lora grinned at him and shook her head. 'I know your game, Luc, and if you think I'm coming anywhere near you while there's the possibility of breakfast downstairs you are very much mistaken.'

'I thought you had a big heart, *mademoiselle*,' Luc said mock-tragically.

'No,' replied Lora. 'Just a big appetite.'

He caught her hand and pulled her to him. 'Lora, will you promise me something?'

'What?' she asked, looking up into his eyes, and feeling a momentary chill at the look in them.

'It's Julie,' he said. 'I can't really explain it all to you now, but she may say some pretty strange things to you today and it would be a good idea if you didn't pay any attention to them. Maybe even if you could avoid her altogether.'

'Avoid her?' said Lora incredulously. 'She's down by the pool having breakfast. Anyway,' she added, her chin lifting, 'what are you so afraid that she's going to tell me?'

'It's to do with business,' said Luc.

'Not about you and her?' she forced out, her heart thudding.

His fingers stroked her face. 'No. Nothing about that. I promise you. There is nothing to tell.'

'Well, what's going on, then?' demanded Lora. 'What business things?'

'About the château,' replied Luc briefly. 'I cannot explain fully now. I have some urgent phone calls to make. You will have to trust me.'

Lora opened her mouth to say something, but before she could frame the words he kissed her on the cheek and strode to the door. Turning, he looked at her and grinned. 'Do not look like that, chérie; I will explain everything as soon as I can. I am not some sort of Bluebeard, so trust me.'

'That's probably what he said,' retorted Lora. 'But I want to know exactly——'

'Sorry,' he said. 'Really I have no time. I have to call New York and the person I want will probably be in bed. Try to have breakfast when Julie has gone. We'll go into town later when I sign the contracts.'

Lora's eyes narrowed, but he was gone. Of all the high-handed, arrogant... Who exactly did he think he was, ordering her about? Knotting the tie savagely around her waist, she made her way outside.

When she arrived at the table by the pool a few minutes later, Julie looked up at her as if she had never seen her before. 'Oh, hi,' she said abstractedly. 'I was just looking at these plans.'

Lora helped herself to a croissant and looked at her questioningly.

'For the château,' explained Julie. 'I expect Luc's explained it all to you.'

'A bit,' said Lora guardedly.

'He's signing the deal today. I don't quite know how he's pulled it off against someone like Mark Todd. Still, I guess you could say Luc regards business opportunities in the same way Captain Kidd viewed passing ships: take what you want and damn the consequences.'

'Mmm,' said Lora non-committally. 'Well, perhaps Luc has slightly more of a sense of right and wrong than Captain Kidd.'

Julie looked at her pityingly. 'Honey, you really can't have known him very long if you think that. When I look at him orchestrating a take-over bid, you know what I think of?'

'Money?' said Lora innocently.

'A killer shark,' replied Julie. 'And with about as much mercy. Luc goes all out for what he wants, and what he wants he gets. Nothing, absolutely nothing, is allowed to stand in his way.'

Lora gazed at Julie's face and sensed a growing unease. Luc's parting words came back to her with startling clarity. Why had he been so keen to keep her and Julie apart? Was it because Julie was going to tell her some lies—or was it because she was going to tell the truth about him? Truth that Luc didn't want Lora to hear?

She came back from her thoughts to realise that Julie was still talking. 'These plans for turning it into a conference centre look magnificent.'

'Conference centre,' echoed Lora, her heart flopping like a landed fish.

'The château,' said Julie. 'It's all here. There's a golf course too, hotel facilities, you name it. He'll make a fortune on the deal.'

'Deal,' repeated Lora. Had it all been for nothing but money, then? She looked up to see Luc standing behind Julie, his face dark with anger, but before he could speak she said, 'Is this true, Luc, about turning the château into a conference centre and all the rest of it?'

He gave her one burning look and then nodded. 'Yes, it is all true.'

'You're going to make so much money, aren't you, Luc?' said Julie happily.

Lora looked at him in mute appeal and then, when it was obvious that he was going to say no more, said softly, 'You really managed to trick me, Luc, didn't you?'

He stared at her as though his face had been carved from stone. 'I am sorry you had to get mixed up in this, Lora. It would have been better if you had taken my advice this morning and not come down.'

'Better?' said Lora bitterly. 'Do you really think so? At least I know the truth now.'

'You know nothing at all about it,' said Luc flatly.

'Oh, come on, Luc,' said Julie, listening with interest to their row. 'We all know how economical you can be with the truth when the situation demands it.'

She turned to Lora and shrugged. 'Sorry, honey, guess you're going to have to do some fast catching up on Luc's ruthlessness. Seems like maybe you don't know him all that well after all.'

Lora didn't pay the slightest attention to Julie. All her senses were tuned to the man standing opposite her. The man she thought she had fallen in love with.

She glared at him and spat, 'You got my sympathy with all that eyewash about the future of the local community and your family honour, and really all you were ever interested in was making a fast buck—just like Mark Todd.'

'What's wrong with that?' demanded Julie, getting to her feet.

'You lied to me,' said Lora, staring at Luc, and then, glancing at Julie, something in her finally snapped.

'Oh, go away and mind your own business, you silly woman,' she said irritably, and pushed her into the pool. Julie fell backwards with a gasp and a splash, still holding on to the plans for the château.

'That's the best thing you've done all morning,' said Luc, his eyes glinting. 'I wish I'd thought of it.'

'You can join her if you like,' snarled Lora. 'I'm just surprised you haven't already dived in to save your precious plans.' She gazed at him bitterly. How could she have been taken in by all his lies? The memories of last night's sweet caresses were like acid in her face. She lifted her chin, her face bleak. 'It's a real pity you know how to swim,' she added.

'Perhaps I should have taken lessons from you,' he drawled. 'You are the expert in throwing yourself in the deep end and thrashing about over things you don't understand.'

'Oh, but I understand all too well,' she replied. 'Correct me if I'm wrong, but I get the strangest feeling that you have just used me to achieve your own ends. Isn't that just the silliest thing?'

Luc strode towards her but Lora stood her ground, her eyes blazing. 'When you kidnapped me, Luc, you told everyone not to believe me when I told the truth. This morning you said exactly the same thing to me about Julie.'

'This morning was different,' grated Luc.

'I'm sorry, but I just don't believe you,' said Lora defiantly. 'How do I know she's not telling the truth too? What possible reason could she have to lie?'

Julie had swum to the edge of the pool now and was hauling herself out of it, her face grim. Mascara was running down her cheeks, her once perfectly ordered hair hanging in rats' tails. Luc glanced at her and then at Lora. She waited for him to say something, anything, to restore her faith in him, but this time there was no magic door for him to open with a flourish.

Her eyes brilliant with tears, she turned and, half running, made for the house. But Luc had caught up with her before she had gone two strides. 'Leave me alone,' she said furiously, trying hard but unsuccessfully to shake him off.

'No,' said Luc. 'I want to talk to you.'

'We have nothing to discuss,' grated Lora. 'I hope your conference centre makes you very happy.' She glanced at Julie, who was gasping by the edge of the pool. 'Don't you think you ought to go and give her a swimming lesson?' she said acidly.

'Julie doesn't need any lessons in survival,' he replied grimly, piloting Lora through the front door and out towards the Mercedes.

'You understand that I'm only getting in this car because I need a lift to town. I want to head straight for the airport,' she said, her heart thudding at the sure knowledge that Luc was holding back his anger only with the maximum of effort.

He flashed a burning look at her, slid into the driver's seat, started the engine and pulled out on to the open road. 'The taxi for that journey left last night, Lora. We have unfinished business to attend to.'

'Not in town,' she retorted. 'And not with you.'

'You forget,' he said softly, 'I am signing for the château this morning, and nobody, not even you, is going to stand in the way of that.'

'I wouldn't be too sure,' flared Lora. 'I work for the opposition, remember? And if I can do anything to make up for my stupidity of the last few days, then I will.'

'If you decide to throw yourself out of the car,' ground out Luc, 'you know where the handle is, but don't expect me to stop for you this time.'

'Oh, no, Luc,' said Lora softly. 'I don't want to run away from you. I'm going to stick just as close as I can, and if I can get my revenge for the way you've treated me I will, don't you doubt it.'

He flashed her a glance. 'If I were not in such an appalling hurry, do you know what I would do?'

Lora took in the grim lines of his face and the savage twist to those full lips. Why did she have to keep provoking this man, when the sensible course would be to say nothing at all?

'What?' she quavered, and then, swallowing, repeated more huskily, 'What, Luc? Just what would you do?'

His eyes were back on the road now, the speed of the car edging towards eighty. 'I would take my revenge on you, Lora, for being unable to accept that I could just have my reasons for not telling you the whole truth.'

Glancing at her set face, he shrugged and added, 'The trouble is, if last night was anything to go by, we would both enjoy it too much. But maybe then you would be calm enough for me to explain this whole mess to you, down to the last tiny infuriating detail.'

'You can explain until you are blue in the face,' retorted Lora. 'I will never believe a word you say ever again.'

'If you had done as I asked and not spoken to Julie this morning, we would not now be having this argument,' replied Luc.

'If I had done as you asked,' said Lora coldly, 'I would never have found out the truth. Julie, although I dislike her intensely, did me a big favour by talking to me.'

'So that's why you pushed her in the pool,' Luc remarked drily. 'I must remember never to do you any favours.'

Lora coloured. 'I couldn't help it,' she said at last. 'She just doesn't seem to know when to stop talking sometimes.'

'She certainly does far more talking than is good for her,' grated Luc.

'She said you always got what you wanted, no matter what,' said Lora. 'And then when she started talking about your plans for the château I could see that she was right. You kidnapped me, without a thought really for how that would affect me. I expect you made love to me last night merely because I happened to throw myself at you.'

She looked straight out of the window, her hands twisting in her lap, before she added, 'And I expect the only reason you made love to me this morning was to keep me away from Julie.'

Luc screeched to a halt, a juggernaut coming right up behind them and then overtaking at the last moment with a blare of horns and a squeal of tyres. 'You really have a high opinion of me, don't you?' he said dangerously.

'You kidnapped me,' flared Lora, 'and you told me a pack of lies. What am I supposed to believe?'

'Who would you rather believe?' said Luc harshly. 'Me or Julie?'

'I would rather believe you,' said Lora in a low voice. 'But I don't know how I can.'

'Then after I have signed the contract for the château I will take you to the airport and we will have done with this silliness,' Luc bit out. 'You can go home to your career opportunity and your lover and forget everything that ever passed between us.'

Lora felt as though her heart was being torn in shreds. 'Perhaps I'll just have you sent to prison,' she blazed. 'Maybe then you won't be so arrogant.'

A tractor pulled out in front of them and Luc leant on the Mercedes' horn. Lora suddenly thought again of jumping out of the car and glanced down at the door-handle. Maybe if he did drive on and leave her it would be better for all concerned.

'Don't even think it,' said Luc wearily, as if he could read her thoughts exactly. 'You escaped that first attempt with a few bruises. This time you might break something.'

He'd already broken her heart; what else was there that mattered? 'Much as you'd care,' flashed Lora. 'You said you'd leave me lying in the road.'

Luc shrugged. 'There is a heavy fine for littering the public highway. And besides,' he added with a grim smile, 'the garage was good enough to mend the central locking and I have activated it.'

It was market day and the town was bustling with people. Luc parked the car as near to the centre as he could get. 'Come,' he said. 'We have a little time yet. Let's go to a café. Maybe we can begin to sort this muddle out.'

'Why should I want to go anywhere with you?' demanded Lora.

Luc regarded her calmly. 'Firstly because the temperature in this car, left in the sunshine, will soar over a hundred degrees and I have no wish to be responsible for roasting you to death. And secondly,' he added, taking her hand, 'because, however much we shout at each other, occasionally we need to talk.'

'We haven't got anything to talk about,' said Lora stiffly.

Luc sighed. 'If you don't come and have a sensible conversation with me right now, Lora Seaton, I shall pull you over into the back seat and make love to you.'

Lora looked at the gendarme standing near the car, and all the people going by. 'You wouldn't dare,' she breathed, only too well aware that this man would dare do anything to get what he wanted. 'What about all this stuff about you being a respectable pillar of the local community?'

'Even pillars can crumble eventually,' replied Luc.

The café was crowded but they seemed to be served almost as soon as they sat down at the little marble-topped table on the pavement. Nearly everyone going past waved or had something to say to Luc, and it was difficult for them to have any sort of conversation without being continually interrupted.

'Lora,' he began at last, 'I know it's difficult talking here, but you have completely the wrong idea about what is going to happen to the château. I shall be signing for it in a few minutes and I should like to believe, while I do, that I have your support.'

'Are you turning it into a conference centre?' demanded Lora. 'Is there going to be a golf course with "foolish tourists" wandering across it? Are the vines going to be grubbed up?'

Luc gazed at her. 'Tell me something, Lora, before I answer your questions.'

'What?' she said grudgingly.

'Why does it matter to you what I do to the place? Why do these ideas affect you so strongly?'

Lora looked him straight in the eye. 'Because you led me to believe that you cared about these places, about the countryside, and the people.' She wanted to add, And about me, but did not have the courage. She swallowed and then resumed, 'And I fell...' This was no good at all. Biting her lip, she said, 'I grew to like you, Luc, on the basis of that. That you would fight for what you believed in. That you cared.' She shrugged. 'It may sound silly, but it didn't seem so bad being your captive when it was a means to an end. And now I find that you're really only fighting for a profit, and that was why you lied to me and used me. And I wonder if, really, you cared about me at all.' She stopped then, simply unable to go on.

'Lora,' he said gently, reaching out an arm to pull her close.

'Don't "Lora" me,' she said fiercely, jumping up as if his touch burned her. 'I'm going to wash my face.' Well aware that people were looking at her tear-stained features, she turned on her heel and fled to the lavatories.

It was while she was looking at her face in the cracked mirror of the ladies' loo that she saw the small window above one of the cubicles. It would be a perfect way to escape from this whole mess.

As quick as thought she bolted herself in and then, standing on the toilet seat, she got one foot on the cistern and the other knee on the window-ledge. She could just do it. With one desperate heave she manoeuvred herself through the opening and landed in a quiet alley beside some dustbins.

Her first thought as she brushed herself down was to find a telephone. She would ring Mark and tell him what had happened. He deserved that much, despite the way he had behaved towards her. And then, when she had told him, she would resign. She had been going to do that anyway, after her French trip. It had been pointless thinking that she could continue working for a man who had acted as he had. Strange how she had lied to Luc that she and Mark were lovers. Nothing could be further from the truth.

She raked her fingers through her hair. She had to hurry. Luc would not spend a great deal of time waiting tamely for her to return.

The telephone kiosk, when she found it, seemed not too different from the ones in Britain. But try as she might she could not get the damn thing to work.

'You need to insert some money before you can do anything, Lora. Even if you just want to ring the operator.' A voice she had almost forgotten broke into her thoughts. She whirled around to find Mark Todd standing beside her, a dangerous smile on his face.

CHAPTER NINE

'MARK!' gasped Lora, stunned by his appearance. 'I was just trying to ring you. Something terrible has happened.'

He raised an eyebrow, and then, his voice laden with sarcasm, said, 'Really? I thought from the phone messages I was getting that you were far too busy taking tourist trips round the countryside to bother getting in touch with me.'

'No, Mark, listen——' she began, but he cut in before she could explain.

'What the hell has been going on, Lora? First you don't ring me, and then when I phone the *notaire* he tells me you never showed up when you were supposed to sign that contract. Do you know how that has snarled up my business?' He stood there in his immaculately cut suit, glaring down his nose at her as if she were some particularly nasty smell. 'And then when I decide to come and see for myself what's been going on,' he continued, 'the hotel tells me you checked out almost as soon as you arrived.'

'I can explain everything,' said Lora breathlessly, 'if you'll just listen to me.'

Mark gazed at her with smiling disbelief. 'Oh, I'll listen all right,' he said softly. 'But your story had better be good, because I have a lot of money riding on this deal.'

Lora looked at him and wondered how she could ever have been taken in by him. 'Money!' she said at last. 'I'm sick to the back teeth of that word. I don't care

155

how much you had staked on this precious property deal. Whatever has gone wrong with it is absolutely nothing to do with me.'

'You work for me, remember?' he snarled. 'Signing the contract was your responsibility, Lora.'

'It wasn't one I could do much about,' she said coldly, 'even with the best will in the world, seeing that Luc kidnapped me.'

Mark literally took a step back, the alarm on his face only too obvious. 'Luc de la Falaise is back? I thought he was taking six months off travelling in South America.'

'He came back when his father and brother died in a car crash,' said Lora shortly. 'He found out all about you lending them money and then trying to foreclose on the deal. And then he decided to kidnap me to stop me signing the contract on your behalf.'

'I don't believe you,' said Mark. 'Why should he kidnap you when he could just bribe you?'

'Maybe I'm not bribable,' said Lora, remembering Luc's assessment of her character.

'Everybody is bribable,' scoffed Mark. 'How much did he pay you to cheat me?'

'He didn't pay me anything,' replied Lora wearily. 'That's all you can think about, isn't it? Money.'

Mark glared at her disbelievingly. 'If you're a kidnap victim, what are you doing wandering about the streets making telephone calls?'

'I escaped,' bit out Lora. 'And believe it or not I was trying to phone you.'

'Well, I'm here now,' replied Mark. 'Where exactly is Luc?'

'Do you want to know so that you can face him, or avoid him?' asked Lora coldly.

'Of course I don't want to face him,' Mark replied impatiently. 'What do you take me for?'

'Something very low down on the scale of evolution,' said Lora tartly. 'And I have done ever since that evening at La Cupole.'

Mark shrugged. 'That was your fault for being so naïve.'

'You told me you wanted to take me for dinner because you felt so grateful towards me for going to France in your place,' ground out Lora. 'You said you had last-minute things to discuss with me. Why shouldn't I have agreed to meet you?'

Mark made a dismissive motion with his hands. 'Look, I don't have time to discuss your foolishness now.'

Lora glared at him. 'Well, I do. And if you want to find out where Luc is you'll have to listen to me.'

Mark grabbed her wrist, but she shook him off. 'Oh, no, you don't. That was what you tried in the restaurant, remember? And more besides. You're the creepiest boss I've ever had to contend with, Mark Todd. And I take great pleasure in resigning, as of now.'

He stared at her as though he hadn't heard a word she had said. 'Where is Luc, Lora? Stop messing around; I want to know.'

Her eyes widened as realisation of what was going on came flooding back. 'Oh, my God. He's signing the contract this morning. But he could still be in that café searching for me. If you want to get your hands on the château, you'd better get to the *notaire* before he does.'

'You'd better be telling the truth, Lora, or I'll make you regret it,' said Mark, and she could not help the cold shiver that crawled down her spine at his words.

'I wouldn't tell you this at all except that Luc lied to me too,' said Lora abruptly. 'Don't think I'll rush to do you any favours in the future.'

'This one will do quite well for now,' he said, grabbing her by the hand and starting off at a run for the French lawyer's. 'Lucky I know the way,' he added, 'otherwise we'd be in deep trouble.'

Lora tried to wrench her hand away but his grip was like a vice. Several times she tripped and almost stumbled. She felt that, if she had fallen, Mark would not have stopped; he would merely have carried on, dragging her behind him. She could feel her breath rasping in her throat and the sweat running down her neck at the effort she made to keep up, but Mark took no notice; he ran like a man possessed through the market crowds, ignoring the shouts as he barged into people too slow to get out of his way.

At last they plunged down the side-street to the *notaire*'s office, both of them pausing for a moment outside the door, their chests heaving from the effort they had made. Then Mark gripped the handle and Lora was suddenly washed by a feeling of sadness so strong, it almost overwhelmed her. Luc would still be at the café now, waiting for her, while she had led Mark to claim the prize both men so desperately coveted.

But before Mark could turn the handle the door opened, and Luc stood there on the threshold gazing at them, a bitter little smile playing on his face.

'Well, well,' he mused. 'Mark Todd. I cannot say it is a pleasure to meet you, but I am glad you are here all the same. You cannot know how much of a pleasure it gives me to tell you that you are far too late to sign the contract. The château and all its lands are once more under my control, thanks to your assistant, of course.'

Lora reddened, but said nothing.

Mark stared at Luc for a long moment and then shrugged. 'I shall take legal advice, of course.'

'Naturally,' agreed Luc, 'and then you will drop the whole matter.'

'Perhaps,' Mark replied. 'But I might be able to claim you got the contract through unfair and illegal practices. I shall get on to my lawyers as soon as I get back to England and then we shall see.'

Luc gazed at him. 'The only thing you will see is that it would be better if you did not try to provoke me any longer,' he said evenly. 'If I were you I would get out of town right now.'

Mark shrugged. 'Suit yourself, but I wouldn't rest easy just yet.' Then, turning to Lora, he asked, 'How about a drink, Lora? If you've forgotten that unfortunate incident at La Cupole, I might be persuaded not to sack you. He looked at her keenly and then added, 'I might give you a bonus too, if you were prepared to testify that Luc had held you against your will so that you couldn't sign the contract for the château.'

Lora knew Luc was watching her but she could not return his gaze. How many times had she threatened to report him to the police? And now here was Mark offering her the opportunity for revenge on a plate . . .

She lifted her chin and stared at Mark, her eyes flashing. 'The words haven't been invented for how I feel about you, Mark Todd. And you can't sack me. I resigned ten minutes ago.'

'Oh, baby,' he whistled. 'You can't go yet. Think of what I've got to tell your parents.'

'Tell my parents what?' snapped Lora.

'Well, I'm sure I can think of something,' drawled Mark. 'How about how you threw yourself at me, begged me to have an affair with you? About the exhibition you made of yourself that night at La Cupole?'

Lora was only too well aware that Luc was listening to every word Mark was saying. What must he think? 'If you remember correctly,' she said icily, 'it was not I who threw myself at you, but the other way around. The only reason I made an exhibition of myself, as you put it, was that you made that revolting suggestion about spending the night with you. Personally I thought that bowl of strawberries and cream looked very nice running down your face.'

Mark made a move towards her, his face black. 'Maybe I should finish what I started that night. You're not in London now, girl.'

He seemed almost surprised to see Luc's hand on his shoulder, Luc's eyes staring down at him. 'If you do not want to find yourself and your undoubtedly expensive suit up-ended in that dustbin,' Luc almost murmured, 'then I would turn round and walk away now.'

Mark stepped backwards, but as Luc took his hand away Lora's former boss shook himself free and lunged towards her. She had a jumbled impression of Luc reaching out to stop him and then her fury erupted. Her hand balled into a fist and she hit Mark straight on the chin. He stopped as though someone had switched a light out inside him and toppled back into Luc.

Her eyes sparking, she gave both men one burning glance and turned on her heel. Almost as if it had been on cue, a taxi came trundling up the street and Lora waved it down. 'To the airport,' she ordered breathlessly, feeling her neck prickle at the knowledge that Luc had dropped Mark on the pavement and was almost right behind her.

'Don't try to stop me, Luc,' she said defiantly, turning round to stare at him with a bravado she did not feel. 'Besides, I'm sure you two have a lot to talk over.'

Luc gazed contemptuously at Mark staring groggily at the taxi. 'Oh, we do, you can be sure of that,' he said grimly, and then, as he turned back to her, a slow smile spread across his face. 'What, still here? And I thought you were in such a hurry to go. Please don't let me keep you.'

Lora coloured fiercely. 'I thought——'

'That I was going to try to stop you? Certainly not,' he said cheerfully. Lora looked at him suspiciously. What was he up to now? He put a gentle finger under her chin and lifted her face to his. 'You are a free woman now, Lora Seaton. So I can do nothing more than to wish you *bon voyage.*'

Before she could say anything he had bundled her inside the taxi and given some money and fast French instructions to the driver. Then he leant in through her window. 'I have told him to take you straight to the airport, *chérie*, and I have also warned him you might try to get out before he has properly stopped, so he is going to lock your door and escort you to the check-in desk when you arrive at the airport.'

'How dare you treat me like this, Luc?' she fumed.

'You mean, how dare I let you go?' he corrected her silkily.

'I do not mean that at all,' she said untruthfully. 'I'm only too glad to see the back of you. I just object to being treated like some parcel.'

'But, *chérie*,' he smiled innocently, 'I am not treating you like a parcel. Parcels need to be wrapped up in brown paper and have their addresses written neatly on a label.' He looked at her quizzically. 'Somehow I cannot see you wrapped in brown paper. That is too outrageous, even for you. Besides——' he shrugged '—I worry about you. You could get kidnapped. Anything.'

'But Luc——' she began.

He stopped her lips with a kiss. 'No buts. Now you really must go.' He jerked his head back towards Mark and added, 'I have some particularly nasty litter to deal with.'

Before she could say any more he had banged on the roof of the cab and she was speeding away down the street and out of his life.

The taxi driver was as good as Luc's word. He escorted Lora all the way into the airport, took her up to the check-in desk and stuck by her until she went into the departure lounge. He spoke not one word of English and Lora gave up trying to argue with him.

It was obvious that Luc wanted her gone, and there was no way she was going to avoid her flight to England. Not that she didn't want to go home, she reminded herself hurriedly. What was there to stay in France for?

When her flight was eventually called she realised, with a jolt of surprise, that she was being ushered into the first-class section of the plane. She showed her ticket in some confusion to the stewardess, who smiled at her.

'Your ticket has been upgraded, Miss Seaton, did you not know?'

'I...I forgot,' replied Lora hurriedly, sitting down in the big window-seat she was allocated. Luc's doing, of course, she realised. He must have had it changed when he took it from her handbag.

'Champagne?' said the stewardess.

Lora, still looking out of the window, was about to shake her head when her whole body stilled in surprise. Someone was lowering himself into the seat next to hers. Someone with a body she thought she would never see again and a voice which was saying, 'Yes, and one for me too, please.'

'Luc,' she breathed. 'How did you get here?'

'By car,' he said. 'You didn't really think I'd let you go home alone, did you?'

'Why not?' she shrugged. 'The way you packed me into that taxi, I thought you couldn't have been more in a hurry to get rid of me.'

He sighed. 'Really, Lora. I despair sometimes. You have so little faith.'

She glared at him. 'Are you at all surprised?'

The stewardess arrived with the champagne and Luc handed Lora's to her, studying the bubbles in his own as if they were the most interesting things he had ever seen.

'I read somewhere that you're not supposed to drink on aeroplanes,' said Lora at last. 'Something to do with the cabin pressure.'

'You are full of these handy tips,' commented Luc. 'How to deal with kidnappers, practical advice on murder and mayhem, the etiquette of in-flight drinking— and yet you do not take the slightest bit of notice of any of them yourself.' He watched her nervously gulp her drink and added, 'See what I mean?'

'I can't help it,' she admitted. 'I don't like flying and you make me nervous.'

'Aren't you even the slightest bit pleased to see me?' he murmured.

Lora took another gulp of champagne. 'I'm glad you got your château back,' she said at last. 'When are you planning to reopen it as a country club and start raking in all that money?'

His hand closed over hers as it lay on the arm-rest, and she jumped involuntarily, spilling the remains of her champagne. He took the glass away and stared intently into her eyes. 'We need to talk, Lora.'

'We haven't anything to talk about,' she said woodenly.

'Oh, but we do,' he said softly. 'And this couldn't be a better time or place. You can't leap out of the window, stop the plane or reverse it backwards into the control tower.'

'I can always put my fingers in my ears,' she retorted.

His hands closed over both of hers. 'No, Lora, I think you will want to listen to what I have to say.' And he buried his face in the palms of her hands. Her pulse was beating unsteadily and, looking up, he smiled at her. 'You see, I knew you were glad to see me.'

'Don't be ridiculous,' she countered jerkily.

'Would you like me to let go of your hands, then?' he said politely.

'No, don't,' she said hurriedly, gripping his fingers. 'I hate it when the plane bumps like this. I know it's only air-pockets but I hate it.'

His fingers tightened comfortingly round hers. 'What am I going to do with you, Lora?' he sighed.

She glanced at his relaxed face and fought down the urge to kiss him. 'You are not going to do anything with me,' she responded tartly. 'I am free, remember? Anyway,' she added uncertainly, 'I won't let you.'

He smiled gently at her. 'Because of what Julie said?'

She nodded and he stroked her solemn face with his forefinger. 'Even though I told you not to believe a word she said?'

Her heart was thudding at his sure touch and she pushed his finger away with an effort. 'As I reminded you this morning, you were once quite prepared to tell everybody not to believe a word I said.'

He stared her straight in the eyes. 'Then I would like to say, once and for all, that, contrary to any impressions you may have, Julie and I are not having an affair and I am not turning the château into a country club.'

Lora shrugged helplessly. 'I saw the plans this morning, Luc. You were right there, looking over Julie's shoulder. You agreed with Julie when I asked you about them. You could have denied it, said it was all a pack of lies, but you didn't. What possible reason have you got for saying one thing then and another now?'

'Simply because I couldn't tell the truth this morning,' said Luc.

'Well, tell me the truth now,' she said. 'I'm listening.'

He looked at her assessingly and then sighed. 'You are only listening for what you want to hear, Lora. You do not want to believe me, and what I have to tell you is so complex it sounds ridiculous.'

'So you're not going to bother feeding me any lame excuses, then?' she challenged.

He shrugged. 'I think I will wait until we get to England and you can believe the evidence of your own eyes.'

'I believed the evidence of my own eyes this morning,' said Lora tartly.

'*Touché*,' smiled Luc. 'You know, you are the most devastatingly difficult woman to persuade. It must come from working with Mark Todd.' He smiled again as if at a very pleasant memory and Lora looked at him suspiciously.

'What happened to him?'

'Who?' said Luc innocently.

'You know very well who I mean,' said Lora. 'Mark. Where is he?'

Luc opened his eyes wide. 'Why do you want to know? Are you thinking of going back to work for him?'

'Certainly not,' she snapped. 'I just thought you might have done something terrible to him and I don't want to be sitting next to some sort of fugitive from justice when the police arrive. As they most undoubtedly will.'

His eyes sparked with humour. 'If I were a fugitive, Lora, I would have brought along my false moustache. But you are wrong; I have not done anything terrible to Mark Todd.'

Lora was conscious of a vague feeling of disappointment. 'Oh,' she said uncertainly.

'No,' he added. 'I have merely sent him on a long holiday.'

'What do you mean?' she demanded.

He shrugged. 'He was not feeling very alert after you gave him your resignation, Lora, so I took him to the airport and put him on a plane to South America.' He smiled again at the memory. 'The beauty of it is,' he added, 'that I gave him my return ticket so he will have to pay for his own flight back.'

'That's outrageous,' said Lora, trying hard to look cross and failing.

'Why?' he enquired. 'Are you really that concerned about your boss?'

'I do not work for Mark any longer,' retorted Lora. 'I resigned this morning.'

'So I gathered,' replied Luc drily. 'I believe most people use pen and paper when they want to terminate their employment. But in this case I have to applaud your decision to let him have it straight on the chin.'

'He provoked me,' muttered Lora.

Luc raised an eyebrow. 'In that case I must definitely get a gum shield,' he mused. 'And perhaps one of those strange helmets you see boxers wearing when they are training. Tell me, are there even now on the streets of London legions of your ex-bosses staggering about nursing their chins because you decided to hand in your notice literally?'

'I've never punched anyone in my life before,' said Lora fiercely. 'But I could make it a habit if you like.'

Luc held his hands up in mock-appeal. 'Whoa, steady there, I——' But whatever he had been going to say was lost as the plane hit another air-pocket and Lora was thrown into his outstretched arms.

'I could get to be a real supporter of non-violence if this is what it means,' he said softly in her hair.

'You could let me go,' Lora struggled.

'Tell me why I should,' he returned, kissing her lightly on the lips.

'Because everybody is looking,' hissed Lora.

'I don't care,' said Luc. 'Your guard's down and I'm going in for round two.' And, tightening his arms around her, he claimed her mouth as his own. It was no use; Lora could not fight this man. As she had found before, one touch from him and she went up in flames. Without thought of where she was or what else was happening, she gave herself up to his embrace.

'Well,' he said, drawing back at last and gazing at her with those smoky eyes. 'A kiss for now, and we will have so much for later.'

'I don't know what you mean,' she said, colouring.

'You know exactly what I mean,' he contradicted her.

'I don't trust you, Luc,' she said in a low voice. 'There's not going to be any later for us.'

He raised his eyebrows. 'I would never have taken you for such an untrustworthy woman, Lora.'

'I am not untrustworthy,' she bit out. 'It is I who do not trust *you*.'

'Forgive me,' Luc said, with a glint in his eye. 'My mistake. My English, you know.'

'My English, my eye,' retorted Lora.

'Another interesting expression I should learn,' he remarked. 'Perhaps, now you are looking for employment, I could take you up on that suggestion of being my English teacher.'

'It was your suggestion,' retorted Lora. 'And your English is perfectly good enough when you want it to be. You just say these things to wind me up. Just as you are winding me up over Julie and the château and everything else you have lied to me about.'

His fingers gripped hers so hard that she gasped. 'I am not lying to you, Lora,' he said. 'You have my word now, and when we get to England I shall prove it to you.'

'When we get to England,' she snapped, 'I am going straight home and I am going to have nothing more to do with you.'

He smiled at her. 'When we get to England you are coming out for dinner with me, and I will make you eat your words.'

Lora glared at him and turned back to the window. Just because her heart had almost burst through her ribcage when he'd kissed her, it didn't mean that he was any good for her. On the contrary, he made her feel more confused and angry and altogether churned up than any other man she had ever met. Last night had to have been an aberration. That was all. He was so infuriating that she simply couldn't have fallen for him.

At last the plane landed and taxied to a halt outside the terminal building. Lora gave a shaky sigh of relief at the idea of being safely on earth once more and then realised Luc was still holding her hand.

'You can let go now,' she said tartly. 'We've landed.'

He gazed at her innocently. 'But I can't do that, Lora. It is I who am nervous now.'

'You, nervous?' she scoffed. 'You haven't got any nerves to be nervous with.'

'Oh, but I am,' he said softly, drawing her hand through his arm and holding it more securely. 'I'm nervous of what you might do now. I mean, the after-effects of champagne and the fear you have of flying—you could suddenly stand up and try to get away from me. And that would be a terrible thing.'

'I do want to stand up and get away from you, Luc,' she said crossly, her heart beating in an entirely different rhythm from the one she was used to. 'I told you, I'm going to go home and I never want to see you again.'

'We can go to your home if you like, *chérie*—I should like to see where you live,' he agreed. 'But, as I said, you are coming out with me tonight.'

'I shall scream,' she threatened. 'And you will be eating your dinner in a police cell tonight.'

He smiled at her. 'If you try to scream then I shall merely kiss you again. We both enjoyed the last one so much, it would be nice to have another.'

'You are impossible!' she retorted.

'Then that makes two of us,' he replied, taking her into his arms once more.

'What will people think?' she objected feebly, only too well aware that the other passengers filing out of the plane were smiling at Luc's behaviour.

Luc shrugged. 'Who cares what they think? That we are lovers, what else? In any case I do not want to kiss them; it is you I want.' And, bending his head, he kissed her once more.

'Now,' he said, drawing back at last, 'I think it is time we got off the plane, before they fly us somewhere else.' And, taking her elbow in the friendliest-seeming fashion, he escorted her so tenderly out of the aircraft that the stewardesses smiled at each other.

For one second as he piloted her through Customs Control she caught an officer's eye and opened her mouth. But she closed it again without saying anything.

'Well?' said Luc gently. 'This is a perfect time to carry out your threat to scream, Lora.'

She stared at him crossly. 'Maybe I don't want to.'

He smiled, his fingers stroking the inside of her arm. 'Attagirl,' he murmured.

'Don't "attagirl" me,' she retorted. 'I might just change my mind.' But in truth, although she hated to admit it, the temptation just to let Luc take over was overwhelming.

The events of the last few days had left her feeling exhausted. The last thing she wanted was a fuss in a public place—which she was absolutely sure Luc was far more equal to than she.

'Where are we going?' she demanded as he piloted her out of the terminal building.

'To get a taxi,' he said. 'I thought you said you wanted to go home?'

Surprised, she looked at him. 'I thought you had other plans?'

He shrugged. 'But you are so implacable, Lora. Maybe I have decided to give in, do the decent thing—see you home and forget everything that has happened. After all, you do not believe a word I have said to you. So why should I continue with such a lost cause?' He ushered her into a waiting taxi.

'You know very well why I don't believe you,' retorted Lora, all her suspicions brought to the fore at the innocent look on his face. 'What are you doing?' she yelped as his hand closed over hers.

'I am holding your hand,' he said. 'I thought you might be nervous of taxis as well as planes.'

'Well, I'm not,' she replied, trying without success to pull her hand away.

'Besides,' added Luc equably, 'you might decide to throw yourself out. And that would be a terrible waste.'

Once back at her flat, Lora rummaged in her handbag in vain for her keys.

'What's the matter?' enquired Luc.

'My keys,' she said wildly. 'They're gone. What am I going to do?'

Luc's eyes glinted. 'Break in?' he suggested quietly.

'I live six floors up,' said Lora bitterly. It was all just too much.

'There is only one thing you can do,' said Luc, taking charge. 'You will have to come with me.'

He was greeted like an old friend when he entered the five-star hotel in London's West End. 'Oh, yes, sir, we got your booking,' confirmed the desk clerk. 'Double suite overlooking Green Park. Here is your key, sir.'

'Double suite?' hissed Lora as they got into the lift. 'You've engineered all this, haven't you, Luc? I bet you even pinched my keys.'

Luc gazed at her for a long moment, and then shrugged. As if in answer he took her keys out of his pocket and looked at them interestedly.

'Give them to me,' she said urgently.

'Tomorrow,' he said, holding them out of her reach. 'But for now I should like to know which is the one that opens your heart?'

She coloured and looked away. 'I'm not telling you, and you'll never find it, Luc. That's for sure.'

CHAPTER TEN

As THE bellboy closed the door to their suite and left them in peace, Lora picked up a leaflet about the hotel and stared over the top of it at Luc. It was silly how attracted she was to him. He had kidnapped her and lied to her and treated her with infuriating arrogance, but there was a devastating charm about him that she just could not ignore.

In fact, if she was going to be honest with herself, there wasn't really anything about him that she didn't like, she found herself thinking dreamily, although she wasn't going to let him know that. Not yet, anyway.

She gazed at his face, taking in each feature separately as if she was cataloguing it forever, and then, as she moved her attention to his eyes, the expression in them made her stop dead.

'What are you looking at?' Lora demanded quaveringly.

'You,' he replied simply, and then, holding out his arms, added softly, 'Come here.'

She dropped the pamphlet on the floor and held his gaze. 'Why should I?' she said softly.

'Because it's right,' he answered, reaching out his arms and drawing her close. 'This will never do, Lora,' he murmured huskily. 'I thought you had decided you wanted nothing more to do with me?'

'I thought so, too,' she admitted. 'I guess I'm just too weak-willed to resist you properly.'

'What about this evening?' he said. 'How far are you going to resist me on that?'

'So you really are determined to go through with all this "proof"?' she said.

'Of course,' he said calmly. 'You must see for yourself the complexities of what I have been dealing with.'

Somehow she had expected him to drop the subject when they got to London, to continue to fob her off. And, she knew ruefully, she would almost have been prepared to put up with it, to ignore reality for the sake of having Luc near. His honesty disarmed her and she stared at him for a long moment before shrugging helplessly. 'I have nothing to wear,' she replied. 'We could just stay in, I suppose.' Suddenly an evening in with Luc, despite everything he had done, held a great allure.

But he looked down at her and shook his head. 'Not tonight, Cinderella,' he said. 'Tonight you shall go to the ball. We will go downstairs and pick something elegant and extravagant for you to wear.'

At the shop in the hotel lobby Lora gasped at the price-tags, but Luc seemed not in the least bit fazed. 'What about this one?' he suggested, holding out a blue taffeta creation.

Lora looked at it assessingly, but before she could speak a bellboy entered. 'Phone call for you, sir.'

Luc thrust the dress into her hands. 'I'm not sure how long I'll be, Lora. Choose what you like and put it on my account.' Smiling encouragingly at her, he hurried away.

Lora gazed again at the blue dress slithering over her hands. It was lovely, that was certainly true, but it was not exactly the thing to set a man's heart on fire.

She raised her eyes to the window, which fronted Piccadilly, and gasped. What she had just glimpsed outside couldn't be true. It simply couldn't. Dropping the dress on the floor, she hurried closer to the window to see Luc and Julie crossing the street and entering a pub together. She watched stupefied as Luc waited for Julie to enter first, his hand lightly resting on the small of her back.

Stunned, she turned from the window and sat down on the little chair by the counter. What was she going to do? Her first reaction was simply to run away, but she couldn't go home. Luc had her keys. She stared unseeing at the blue taffeta.

'Are you all right, miss?' She looked up dully to find the shop assistant gazing at her in concern.

'Yes,' she replied slowly. 'I'm all right.' And then added helplessly, 'But this dress isn't.' Lora looked vaguely around the shop until her eyes were caught by a flash of red and, her resolve hardening, a sudden wicked desire overwhelmed her. 'What about that dress over there?' she suggested. 'That red strapless one.'

Some time later she had decided on the dress, bag, shoes and costume jewellery. If Luc wanted to play games with her she was going to prove herself more than equal to the challenge. 'How much?' she enquired, determined to pay for it all herself.

'Oh,' said the assistant, disconcerted for the first time. 'I've put it all on Monsieur de la Falaise's account.'

Lora glanced sharply at the girl and knew from her face that it was being taken for granted that she was Luc's mistress. The assistant held out the receipts and Lora went pale green. 'That much, huh?' she managed to croak. And then she smiled bitterly. 'Well, I don't much care if he does get the bill,' she bit out. 'I expect the first day's profits from his rotten country club will cover it.'

She returned, with a thumping heart, to the suite. What would happen if she found Luc and Julie inside? She felt sick at the images her brain was conjuring up, but when her trembling fingers turned the key there seemed to be no one there at all.

And then a floorboard in the bedroom creaked and, her heart in her mouth, she whirled around. Luc was standing in the doorway, naked except for a towel around his waist. He smiled at her and opened his arms. 'I missed you,' he said simply. 'Come here.'

She took a step backwards and he frowned. 'What's the matter?' he said softly. 'You look like you've seen a ghost.'

It was on the tip of her tongue to tell him what she had seen, to accuse him again of two-timing her, and then the memory of the previous night swamped her. She couldn't go through all that again. She would just pick a moment and leave without saying anything. It would be better that way.

Trembling, she put a hand to her face. 'I'm just tired,' she said. 'I expect you jolted me, appearing like that.'

He smiled at her. 'I'm not surprised you're tired,' he said. 'You need a good rest. Preferably by the pool of some French farmhouse. I can recommend the perfect one.'

She smiled lop-sidedly at him and sat down limply in one of the armchairs. How could he be such a good liar?

'Lora?' he said, concern sharpening his words. 'Are you all right?'

'I told you,' she said wearily. 'I'm just tired.' Her nails dug into the arms of the chair as he stood behind her, his hands rubbing her shoulders.

'I'm just going to get dressed,' he told her. 'And then I have to go out. I was going to ask you to come with me, but I don't think you're up to it.'

'No,' Lora agreed dully, 'I don't think I am,' adding silently, Not now Julie's back. Somehow she just couldn't face any more lies.

He looked at her closely. 'Are you sure you are all right, Lora?'

'Perfectly,' she managed.

He stared at her consideringly and then said, 'I will be back in time to take you to dinner and I think we shall have something to celebrate.'

'Where are you going?' faltered Lora.

'Business,' he said, lifting his hands from her shoulders and going back to the bedroom. 'About the château, and other things. I will tell you all about it later.'

'I bet you will,' muttered Lora to herself. 'Just like you've told me all about Julie.'

She stared out of the window at the beauty of Green Park. It seemed only a few moments before Luc was back, immaculate in a dinner-jacket.

'How do I look?' he grinned.

'As if you're off to meet your lover,' she said lightly, her smile cracking.

He moved swiftly across to her and took her in his arms, his face concerned. 'Are you sure you are all right, Lora? I'm beginning to get worried about how pale you are looking.'

'I'm quite all right,' she managed, her breathing fast and shallow.

'Try to rest while I'm out,' he said. 'And then we can have the rest of the evening relaxing together.'

He kissed her lightly on the lips and with one final encouraging smile made for the door.

'Luc?' Her voice almost cracked as she said his name.

He turned immediately. 'What, *chérie*?'

'Can I come with you, now?'

Was that flicker in his eyes one of concern for her, or his own predicament?

He shook his head. 'Perhaps it is better if you do not, Lora. You look so ill. This business is of a particularly shoddy sort. You would not like it, and——' he shrugged '—I don't think you'd be up to a meeting like this; I feel that you're sickening for something.'

She swallowed, her eyes huge with sadness. 'Yes,' she said as calmly as she could. 'You're probably right. I'll see you later.'

He nodded encouragingly. 'I must go, Lora,' he said. 'See you soon.' And he left.

She stared wretchedly at the door for some time. Now was the perfect moment to leave. That was for sure. Then her eyes fell on the clothes she had bought that afternoon and the desire for revenge flared up in her once more. On the plane Luc had threatened to make her eat her words. Well, now, maybe, she would make him eat his, would show him up so decisively that he couldn't lie his way out.

Her mind made up, she strode to the telephone and called the front desk. 'Oh, yes, hello,' she said to the clerk. 'Monsieur de la Falaise left his suite a few minutes ago, but unfortunately he left some very important papers. Could you tell me where he has gone?'

She raised her eyes to the ceiling at the lies she was telling. The clerk would think she was absolutely bonkers, but it was worth a try. She could hear him talking to a colleague and then he came back on the line. 'Actually, miss, he is in the cocktail bar.'

Lora replaced the telephone and raced into the bathroom. If she had a very quick shower and put her make-up on in record time, she might just catch him yet.

Her fingers trembled as she applied her mascara some twenty minutes later. Now was not the time to lose concentration. She brushed it on as quickly as she dared and hoped the little wobbliness in her eyeliner wouldn't show too much.

She stood back at last and surveyed herself in a full-length mirror, arrested once more by her reflection. Her hair, pulled quickly into a French pleat, suited the simplicity of the dress, which did remarkable things for a figure she hadn't really known she had.

She twisted a handkerchief nervously between her fingers at the thought of going down to the bar on her own. Luc was going to be there, and Julie too, if her suspicions were correct. This time he would have to tell her the truth. Did she really want such a confrontation?

Luc was using her for something, that much was certain, however much he protested his innocence. But he would soon regret he'd ever met her, she told her reflection defiantly. And then she twisted her lips and sighed. It was all very well being brave before the event, but could she really call the shots when Luc was there with her, his body next to hers, his eyes seeking out her soul?

The desk clerk gazed appreciatively at her as she walked slowly down the hotel stairs. People in the lobby turned to look and the busy bar hushed as she entered.

Luc had his back to her and Lora could not help noticing how the beautifully tailored cloth of his jacket accentuated his broad shoulders and narrow waist. He was talking to another man, and Lora stopped in some confusion. This was not what she had pictured happening at all. Where was Julie? She almost turned tail and fled, but as his companion's attention wandered to Lora Luc stopped in mid-conversation and turned around.

She swallowed as his eyes raked over her and then stopped, uncertain whether to go right up to him and slap his face or just run straight back upstairs. But before she could do either Luc made the decision for her.

Putting down his drink, he strode across the bar towards her and caught her hands in his. Oblivious of the attention that everyone in the bar was giving them, he smiled down into her face. 'Lora, are you sure you are all right?'

'As right as I'll ever be,' she said woodenly.

He raised an eyebrow and gazed at her dress. 'It seems you have turned into a scarlet woman. I approve.'

His choice of words made her clench her jaw. 'Scarlet women seem to be your forte, Luc, don't they? I mean, look at the way Julie Woods whisked you off earlier this evening. Where is she now, powdering her nose?' And then in an undertone she added, 'Let go of my hands.'

He grinned lazily at her, only the slightest flicker in his eyes showing any concern at her remarks, and said softly, 'Not on your life, Lora. You are not climbing out of any windows this evening.'

He held her fast as she tugged ineffectually to free her hands, and then added, 'You know, that dress is really quite a feat of engineering. I wish I'd seen you getting into it, but then——' he shrugged '—it will be so much more fun getting you out of it.'

Drawing her close, he led her to the bar, his lover-like pose effectively stopping her from making a run for it. 'Let me go,' said Lora grimly.

'No,' he said. 'You are here now—it would be a pity to miss what is about to happen, although it won't be as much fun as you envisaged.'

'Fun?' she struggled. 'I'd rather be in a bus queue.' This was not turning out at all how she had imagined it. She had wanted to impress, to shock, somehow to humble Luc. But it was like trying to humble the Empire State Building.

'Stop fighting me,' he said gently. 'You can't win this game, Lora. Not tonight.'

'It's not a game to me,' she retorted.

He squeezed her hand. 'Good,' he murmured. 'Now,' he added raising his voice slightly, 'I want to introduce Mr Smith to you.'

Lora looked at the man Luc had been drinking with when she had arrived. He was a particularly nondescript man, she thought, and yet there was more character behind that façade, she felt sure. 'Is that your real name, Mr Smith?' she asked.

He nodded his head ruefully. 'Yes. Not that anybody ever believes me, especially in my line of business.'

'Your——' But before Lora could finish her question Luc interrupted.

'Ah, the fourth member of our party, at last.' And, turning, Lora saw Julie Woods enter the room.

She found herself almost too shocked to speak. So he had arranged to meet Julie. But did Luc think she was just going to sit calmly by while he entertained his other woman? She made an involuntary movement, almost as if she was going to shake Luc off and leave, but his grip tightened round her arm.

'You can't go yet, Lora. This is what you came down for, what you have come to see.'

She glared at him. 'You have a real nerve, don't you? How can you do this, Luc? Is your ego so huge it needs to be fed by upsetting two women?'

Luc grasped her hand and raised her fingers to his lips. 'I can't speak for the size of my ego,' he told her. 'I haven't measured it lately. But you, my dear, seem to have no ego at all. You simply have to believe the worst, don't you?'

Lora swallowed, a huge lump in her throat. 'What else is there to believe in, Luc?'

A faint smile crossed his face. 'Me?' he suggested, and, keeping hold of her hand, he turned to greet Julie, who was walking up to join them.

'Hi, Luc.' The American nodded at Lora. 'Hi.'

Within a very short time Lora, as if in a dream, found herself sitting with the others at a small table. This simply could not be happening, she told herself. It was so... bizarre. Luc must be completely crazy.

He ordered drinks and there was a momentary silence after they arrived, almost as if everyone was having doubts of his and her own about this extraordinary meeting.

Then, unable to bear the tension any more, Lora said the first thing that came into her head. 'I'm sorry I pushed you in the pool today, Julie——' she began, and then stopped, realising how tactless she had been, when she saw the expression on the American's face.

Luc shot Lora an amused glance, but did not say anything to rescue her. He merely raised an eyebrow as if to remark, Go on, then; how are you going to extricate yourself from this?

Lora glared at him and turned back to Julie. 'I really am sorry. I don't know what came over me.'

Julie shrugged. 'Neither do I, honey. Maybe it was all the talk about the plans for the château—I guess it could be a bit unnerving to find the man you're crazy about has been lying to you.'

Lora drew in her breath sharply. That was the last reply she had expected, and to hear her own corrosive doubts mirrored so exactly was like a blow in the face.

She stared at Luc but his eyes were on Julie now, dark, assessing eyes, and when he spoke it was in a calm, measured tone. 'I did not lie to Lora, Julie.'

Julie swallowed some of her drink and gazed at him disbelievingly. 'Oh, yeah? Pull the other one, Luc. And that reminds me,' she went on, as if oblivious of the tension surrounding her, 'that housekeeper of yours—Maria. She has really gone beyond the limit, you know.'

'Maria is almost a member of my family,' grated Luc.

'Well, she certainly doesn't act like a member of staff,' retorted Julie. 'Do you know what she did this morning?' she asked, turning to Lora.

Lora shook her head.

'I asked her to bring me a towel, after you pushed——' Julie stopped. 'After that unfortunate incident by the pool,' she amended with heavy sarcasm. 'And you know what? Admittedly my French isn't too good, but she just turned round and told me to take a hike, in good old-fashioned Anglo-Saxon American.' She glared at Lora. 'And I guess I know where she learnt her new vocabulary, huh?'

'She taught herself,' said Lora acidly. 'And personally I think she used a very good choice of words.'

Luc put his hand over hers and gave it a warning squeeze. 'That's enough,' he said gently. 'I apologise on Maria's behalf, Julie, but I didn't ask you here this evening to talk about her.' He indicated the man sitting next to him and went on, 'I want you to meet Roland Smith, Julie. He's an accountant.'

Was it Lora's imagination or was there a flicker of fear over the American's face at the mention of Mr Smith's occupation? The temperature in the room seemed suddenly to have plummeted and Lora shivered.

Julie looked at the stranger but seemed unable to meet his eyes. 'Pleased to meet you,' she said guardedly.

'Likewise,' nodded Mr Smith with more than a hint of irony. 'I admire your work very much.'

'My w-work?' stumbled Julie. 'I don't know what you mean.'

'Don't you?' said Luc gently. 'I think you know only too well, Julie.'

She half rose from the table, like a wild animal who had suddenly scented danger. 'Sit down,' ordered Luc wearily. 'There is no point in trying to escape, so you might as well hear us out.'

Julie sat.

Lora stared at their faces, all too conscious that the temperature of their meeting was now well below zero. She looked at Julie, who was frightened but defiant, and then at Luc, grim but determined. Mr Smith was almost totally expressionless.

'I think you can guess why I asked you here this evening,' said Luc. 'All that money you've tried to siphon away from my companies and into your own accounts.'

'It's a lie!' burst out Julie.

'No,' said Luc flatly.

He nodded to Mr Smith, who lifted a briefcase to his knee and clicked it open. Taking out a bundle of documents, the accountant looked at Julie and said gently, 'It's all here, miss. You led us quite a dance at first, but we cottoned on to your methods in the end.'

Luc gazed steadily at Julie. 'You thought when I went to South America that it was the perfect opportunity for you to start robbing me blind. And maybe if you had concentrated your efforts and disappeared before I had got back it would have taken me longer to catch up with you.'

'It was the car crash,' said Julie slowly. 'I had everything planned and then you came back.'

Luc nodded. 'Unfortunate for you, but I still read the accounts while I was away. Did you really think that I would just skim through my business reports? I knew what was going on almost immediately; I just couldn't prove who was responsible.'

He turned to Lora. 'That was why you saw Julie with those plans for the château. If you had bothered to take a closer look you would have realised that they were merely copies of the ones Mark Todd had submitted. Mind you——' he shrugged '—I suppose you would have just thought I was stealing his ideas, much as Julie thought I had done.'

'But why did she have them?' said Lora.

'Because I set her up,' replied Luc. 'I asked her to make certain calculations: profit, loss, turnover, et cetera. Told her she would be in complete control of the project. Then I made my own calculations and compared them with hers today.'

Lora felt suddenly breathless. 'So that's why you two were in that pub together today.'

Julie glared at her. 'What else did you think, sweetheart? That I was having an affair with your man?'

Lora coloured. 'I...'

Julie stared at her assessingly. 'You know, when I first met you I thought maybe Luc was lying about you; that you weren't his girlfriend at all.' Lora and Luc exchanged glances but said nothing. Julie continued, 'I had some kind of suspicion you might just be some kind of accountant, checking up on me.' She gazed at Luc. 'But I've really got to hand it to you, I guess—that you could be so taken up by someone and still try to nail me.'

Luc gazed at her idly. 'I have nailed you, Julie. Every single lie you have told, every cent you have stolen from me has all been accounted for, including the money you stashed in accounts here in London.'

Julie blenched. For the first time she looked truly scared. 'But you can't...' she whispered. 'You can't prove anything about those.'

'Oh, but I can,' said Luc. 'It's all in Mr Smith's paperwork, which is just as well, because the English accounts are where you put most of the money, aren't they?'

Julie stood up suddenly. 'I'm going.'

Mr Smith got up too and closed his briefcase with a snap. 'I think you'll find it easier if you come with me,' he said. 'I didn't tell you that I actually work for the Inland Revenue, and we're really very interested in getting a statement from you.'

Julie stared at him.

'It really would be easier,' he said softly.

For one split-second Lora thought Julie was going to make a run for it, but then she shrugged helplessly and let Mr Smith escort her from the room. She did not look back.

Lora smoothed her hands down her dress. 'Somehow this doesn't seem so very appropriate any more,' she said.

Luc's hand closed over hers. 'I'm sorry you had to see that,' he said softly. 'But at least now maybe you'll understand the whole complicated mess. You looked so unwell earlier, I decided to keep you out of it and tell you about it later over dinner.'

Lora smiled shamefacedly at him. 'When I saw you go into that pub today I really did think you had been lying to me all along. And when you seemed so secretive about tonight's meeting I thought you were two-timing me for sure. I feel so awful for not believing you, Luc.'

He shrugged. 'Julie is not a woman who inspires trust. She sows suspicion and confusion wherever she goes, which is why, I suppose, she is such a successful embezzler.'

'Why did you arrange to meet her here?' asked Lora. 'Why not get the Inland Revenue to do it in one of their offices?'

'If I had asked Julie to meet me anywhere more official she would have smelled a rat,' explained Luc. 'She gave me the figures about the château when I met her in the pub today. I just wanted her to confess of her own volition what she had been up to. I needed to convince

Mr Smith, apart from anyone else, that I too was not involved in any fraud.' He sighed. 'The easiest way to get her to do that seemed to be by asking her here. I always stay at this hotel when I am in London. Nothing could have seemed more normal to her.'

'You're an extremely ruthless man, aren't you?' said Lora shakily.

He nodded. 'Yes, I cannot deny that. When I want something I go for it. And when someone attempts to cheat me I take revenge.'

'Is everything always so black and white for you?' she asked.

His eyes glinted. 'No. Not always.' He looked at her dress and added softly, 'Sometimes the best things in life are scarlet.'

His eyes holding hers, he reached into his pocket, took out the keys to her flat and laid them on the table. 'They are yours, Lora. You are finally free of me, if you want to go.'

Her eyes dropped, her fingers nervously pleating the scarlet taffeta of her lap. 'And if I don't?' She trembled.

He put a gentle finger under her chin. 'There are ties stronger than a kidnapper could ever devise, Lora. And you have already bound me with them. Will you marry me?'

She swallowed, drowning in the soft black depths of his gaze. 'We've only known each other a few days,' she said weakly.

'We have the rest of our lives to get to know each other better, my love,' he replied softly. 'So what do you say?'

She looked up at him and smiled suddenly. 'What is there to say, Luc, except *mais oui*?'

MILLS & BOON

Relive the romance with our great new series…

Bestselling romances brought back to you by popular demand

Each month we will be bringing you two books in one volume from the best of the best. So if you missed a favourite Romance the first time around, here is your chance to relive the magic from some of our most popular authors.

We know you'll love our first By Request volume— two complete novels by bestselling author Penny Jordan—*Game of Love* and *Time for Trust*.

Available: August 1995   Price: £3.99

Available from WH Smith, John Menzies, Volume One, Forbuoys, Martins, Woolworths, Tesco, Asda, Safeway and other paperback stockists.

MILLS & BOON

Dangerous desires and vengeful seductions!

Broken promises and shattered dreams...love's wrongs
always beg to be avenged! But revenge has its price,
as each couple in this compelling volume of four
romances soon discovers.

These strongly written love stories come from four
of our top selling authors:

Susan Napier   Rosalie Ash
Natalie Fox   Margaret Mayo

Vengeance is a powerful emotion–especially
in affairs of the heart!

Be sure to get your revenge this summer!

Published: August 1995   **Price: £4.50**

Available from WH Smith, John Menzies, Volume One, Forbuoys, Martins,
Woolworths, Tesco, Asda, Safeway and other paperback stockists.

GET 4 BOOKS
AND A MYSTERY GIFT

Return this coupon and we'll send you 4 Mills & Boon romances and a mystery gift absolutely FREE! We'll even pay the postage and packing for you.

We're making you this offer to introduce you to the benefits of Reader Service: FREE home delivery of brand-new Mills & Boon romances, at least a month before they are available in the shops, FREE gifts and a monthly Newsletter packed with information.

Accepting these FREE books and gift places you under no obligation to buy, you may cancel at any time, even after receiving just your free shipment. Simply complete the coupon below and send it to:

HARLEQUIN MILLS & BOON, FREEPOST, PO BOX 70, CROYDON, CR9 9EL.

No stamp needed

Yes, please send me 4 free Mills & Boon romances and a mystery gift. I understand that unless you hear from me, I will receive 6 superb new titles every month for just £1.99* each postage and packing free. I am under no obligation to purchase any books and I may cancel or suspend my subscription at any time, but the free books and gifts will be mine to keep in any case. (I am over 18 years of age)

2EP5R

Ms/Mrs/Miss/Mr _____

Address _____

_____

_____ Postcode _____

Offer closes 31st January 1996. We reserve the right to refuse an application. *Prices and terms subject to change without notice. Offer only valid in UK and Ireland and is not available to current subscribers to this series. **Readers in Ireland please write to: P.O. Box 4546, Dublin 24.** Overseas readers please write for details.

You may be mailed with offers from other reputable companies as a result of this application. Please tick box if you would prefer not to receive such offers. ☐

mps MAILING PREFERENCE SERVICE

MILLS & BOON

Kids & Kisses—where kids and romance go hand in hand.

This summer Mills & Boon brings you Kids & Kisses— a set of titles featuring lovable kids as the stars of the show!

Look out for
Fire Beneath the Ice by Helen Brooks
in August 1995

Kids…one of life's joys, one of life's treasures.

Kisses…of warmth, kisses of passion, kisses from mothers and kisses from lovers.

In Kids & Kisses…every story has it all.

Available from W.H. Smith, John Menzies, Volume One, Forbuoys, Martins, Woolworths, Tesco, Asda, Safeway and other paperback stockists.